HIRING MORGANA

WITCH OF THE FEDERATION™ BOOK 02

MICHAEL ANDERLE

LMBPN Publishing
PMB 196, 2540 South Maryland Pkwy
Las Vegas, NV 89109

Version 1.00, October 2021
Previously Published as part of the megabook *Witch of the Federation*
ebook ISBN: 978-1-68500-561-0
Print ISBN: 978-1-68500-562-7

THE HIRING MORGANA TEAM

Thanks to our Beta Team

Mary Morris, John Ashmore, Nicole Emens, Robert Brooks, and
Larry Omans

Thanks to our JIT Readers

Angel LaVey
Jeff Eaton
John Raisor
Larry Omans
Misty Roa
Tim Adams

If We've missed anyone, please let us know!

Editor
The Skyhunter Editing Team

*To Family, Friends and
Those Who Love
To Read.
May We All Enjoy Grace
To Live The Life We Are
Called.*

CHAPTER ONE

It was two hours prior to Stephanie receiving her email from Pinnacle Prep and two hours before she would be considered for admission based purely off her public show of magic. The school was located in the "new" Minneapolis.

In 2067, a tornado of epic proportions raged through a power plant to kaleidoscope towers, tubes, and wires into frenzied destruction. The malevolence of the unprecedented storm pounded the ultra-reinforced containment building and critical cooling lines were severed in the devastation. The rods over-heated to melt the nuclear reactor core and steel containment vessel, and howling winds swept the resultant fallout into the environment.

It was, in terms of nuclear timetables, contained relatively quickly given the magnitude of the spread. It was no Chernobyl by any stretch of the imagination, but essentially, all of Minneapolis, Welch, and everyone else within a three-hundred-mile radius had to get the hell out of Dodge. As time progressed, scientists devised a way to separate the radioactive material from the soil and water. The environment wouldn't be anywhere near sustainable again for hundreds of years but that didn't stop the

Federation from renovating and resurging Minneapolis. It was shiny and new.

All the way up at the top of the Pinnacle tower, Dean Chicane stretched his arms and stepped out of his pod. Laura Sheng and Bradly Liles from Marketing waited in his office alongside one woman from the admin sector.

Chicane turned to survey his staff as he stretched languidly once again and focused his mind on the tasks ahead. He was in his middle forties with peppered hair and stood about five-seven with a thin build. His blue Pinnacle sweater with his white button-up and tie tucked beneath it set the perfect tone. He slipped his black shiny loafers on and picked his glass up, put two ice cubes in, and poured two fingers of Scotch. As almost an afterthought, he raised the bottle in a query to the others, but they declined.

He swirled it in his glass, took a sip, and smacked his lips. "This bottle of Scotch is almost one hundred and fifty years old. I found it in the bullshit left here in the city when the Federation cleaned it up. Finders keepers. Now, what do we have on this first human witch girl? Have we contacted her yet?"

Laura pursed her lips and her gaze rolled over Chicane. He smirked as he took a sip of Scotch. "We wanted to check with you first, sir. Her name is Stephanie Morgana and she lives in a Gov-Sub outside of Chicago."

Bradly cleared his throat and clutched his files to his chest. He was fairly new to the position but was a graduate of the school. "It is an investment, of course."

Chicane gestured dismissively with his free hand. "Yes, yes, but she is a golden ticket. We need to jump on the chance to secure the benefit of bringing her to our school before any of our competitors get their grubby little hands on her. Especially Wayside in Alabama. Those freaks…"

The admin flipped through her paperwork. "Stephanie is actually a very gifted young lady. She scored in the high nineties

—the best score in the Midwest on her testing—and apparently showed some sort of magical ability during that time."

The dean made a motion of impatience as he sauntered over to his chair. "So why the hell didn't we grab her from the get-go? We need smart people in here too, not only the money-thick. I would hate to believe that the wealthy have no brain cells and they are all left to those scrounging for breadcrumbs in the ghettos. Then again, if that were true, they wouldn't be there that long, would they?" He snapped his fingers. "Come on, people, this is what I pay you for. Get the students who will make waves and bring more students in. How is that hard?"

The admin glared at the paperwork through her black cat-eye glasses. "Well, sir, to be quite frank…it was the budget. She would have needed a full ride."

Chicane waved her words off, scoffed, and looked at the picture of his wife before he settled his gaze on Laura's legs. "I told you that someday, we would miss a diamond following those rules."

Laura shrugged, walked over, and picked a towel up to blot the dean's forehead. "Everyone does it. To keep up with the stock market and the expected financial rewards, each student is worth a million apiece. That means that right now, there is close to a billion dollars' worth of youth in the building lying there in their pods and learning from the system. Nonetheless, we have an annual budget to adhere to and that is not a bad thing if you remember ten years ago."

The dean waved her hand away. "That was a fluke. A fluke. Who knew the whole lot of them would have issues due to that chemical spill? They tested genius, all one hundred and seventy-eight of them, and had partial tuition. Then, they all simply melted down in the pods. I don't want to talk about it. This girl is gold."

Bradly put his finger up. "If…if I may, sir…"

He rolled his eyes. "Go on."

The marketing exec pulled out a piece of paper and pushed his glasses up his nose. "We can't do more than two percent tuition assistance. And even then, we need to have some skin in the game. Pure scholarship for this girl would have used all the income from other students."

Dean Chicane sighed, pursed his lips, and tapped his fingers on the desk. His gaze shifted to Laura, who stood beside him, and to the others. "But now, we still have a chance?"

Laura smiled evilly. "With the sheer amount of money it should bring in, we are fairly certain that the payoff outweighs the risk. Yes."

He clapped his hands together and chewed on a piece of ice. "That's what I like to hear."

His decision made, he stood and pulled his sports coat on. Laura put her papers down, dusted his shoulders off, and straightened the bottom of the coat. The dean pointed back and forth between the admin and Bradly. "Okay, this is what I want you to do. Make the offer we talked about. But…it is contingent on her proving her identity and capability to throw magic."

Bradly nodded as he wrote it down. He looked up and pushed at his glasses once more. "An…any magic?"

The dean's lip twitched as he held the glass to it. "Any magic. And I want an answer within two hours as we are holding a place. So, push her."

The young man and the admin hurried out of the room. Laura grabbed her things and the dean swallowed his Scotch before he slapped her on the butt. "I want you to make this happen. You know I like it when you make things happen."

Laura pressed her bright red lips together and pushed her dyed blonde hair from her shoulder. She leaned forward to give him the slightest peek down the front of her dress. "That's what you pay me for. The rest is merely overtime."

She winked, grabbed a cube of ice from his glass, and sucked on it as she turned and walked out the door. Chicane chuckled, situated his pants, and rubbed his hands together. "All right, witchy witch, what you got? Show me what you got."

———

Stephanie had printed out the text portion as well as the attachments that came along with it. She had to give them an answer within two hours from the time that the letter had been opened. By now, she was down to one hour, but she wanted to read all the fine print before she signed up for it. There couldn't be any hidden fees or anything that could come back to bite her.

She read out loud to herself, biting her nails as she paced back and forth behind the couch. "IDs, personal items, school transcripts, letter of approval if under the age of eighteen, Federation health screenings up to date. Okay, I have most of this already."

As she walked forward again, a hand gripped her arm and she stopped. Distracted, she looked up slowly to where her parents stood with worried smiles on their faces. "Sorry. I wanted to look at everything before I said okay. You know? Make sure there are no tricks."

"You get your responsible business acumen from me." Her father folded his arms over his chest.

Her mother looked up and over her shoulder at him with puckered lips. "Yeah, right. You haven't made a business deal in twenty years. I'm the ears and hands of this establishment."

He tapped his wife on the shoulder in agreement. As she looked back at Stephanie, he winked and gave his daughter a thumbs-up, which made her giggle. Her mother elbowed him in the stomach and stepped forward to study the sheet with her. "I'm worried you won't be able to put this all together in time."

Stephanie shrugged and pointed at the list. "I have most of it. I had to have my IDs and stuff for school each year because we live in the Gov-Subs."

Her mother's eyes looked tired and she stepped back with a

sigh. She stared at her for a moment and put her hands out. "I just...you're... I didn't realize you could... Oh, for Pete's sake! You're magic?"

"Oh," Stephanie said, a little chagrined because she'd forgotten that little detail in all the excitement. She grabbed her mother's hand and nodded at her father. "Follow me."

She hurried up the stairs to her room and into the closet to open the box. Inside lay two used batteries and one that was as yet unused. She pulled the full one out and turned with it in her hand. Her parents stood in the doorway, leaning on the doorframe.

Turning it right and left, she tapped a small metal piece on the top. "This is the security cap. To open it, you run your finger down this metal insert on the side and click the small notch hidden right...here."

She tapped it and the cap popped out to reveal six slivers of metal that had been embedded in notches in the stone. It hissed as the magic began to flutter through it and the stone's appearance faded, leaving what could be mistaken as a larger glass vial. A small trail of purple haze sifted out of the notches and wound itself down the stone and back up again.

Her mother jumped slightly at the hiss and put her hand on her chest. "And now what do you do?"

Stephanie's eyes glimmered as she moved the stone into her left hand and opened her right. She closed her eyes and whispered the words softly. A small blue flame grew in her palm, flickered to yellow, then green, then red, and back to blue again. She opened her eyes and grinned in satisfaction.

Her parents both walked forward, bent slightly at the waist, and stared in awe at the flame. Her father tilted his head from side to side. "Does it hurt?"

She shook her head. "No. It's not the same kind of fire."

Her mother held her hand a few inches above it, her palm flat.

"It doesn't give off any heat. That is so strange. Does it hurt you to do magic like this?"

Stephanie lifted one side of her mouth in a half smirk. "Not at all. Not this stuff. It can make me a little tired, but nothing other than that."

Her parents stepped back, and she swatted the flame against her leg so the sparkling remnants dissipated. She clicked the security cap back on the battery and put it away in the closet. Her mother looked at her husband and back at Stephanie. "We aren't thrilled that you have engaged with a company without permission, but we also think you need to do what you think is best for you. We'll support any choice you make."

She smiled, pulled the tablet off her bed, and opened the email with the countdown now at twenty minutes. Biting the inside of her lip, she hovered her finger over accept and deny and hoped fervently that she had made the right choice. When it ticked down another minute, she held her breath and pressed accept.

After a quick, sharp breath, she ran forward and hugged them both. "Thank you, guys. This means the world to me. I really thought I would have to go to Asia or steal a pod or something to be able to make these dreams happen. I know it's a risk, but I also know this could mean my way in permanently and that means we could all see a brighter future."

Her mother's mouth curled into a proud smile and she pulled her in to hug her tightly. "That's the girl I know. Never only thinking about herself. But when you go to this school and you are there to learn, the focus needs to be on you and your future. Everything else after that will fall in line so simply. But you need the head start first. You deserve the head start."

Dad came over and joined the hug. "Besides, we really hope we don't have to go into the Federation nursing facilities when we're old and gray. We need you to make the bucks so we can lounge around on that little tiny speck of Georgia that's left. I hear that if you sit there long enough on low tide, you can see some of the old tall buildings from the state of Florida."

Her mother snorted. "And three-eyed fish from the nuclear hell that is the rest of the world."

Stephanie giggled and pulled back to give them each a kiss on the cheek. She held the paper to her chest and bounced up and down excitedly. "I'm going to go call Todd and tell him all about it. He will totally freak. Thanks again. I love you guys."

They stepped aside to let her pass and then back together again and watched her run down the steps. Mark, her father, put his arm around Cindy and pulled her in close. "At least she got my smarts."

His wife didn't respond to his joke. She simply stood there and leaned her head against him, her eyebrows pulled into a small frown. They lingered for several moments and listened to her screech on the messenger call with Todd downstairs. It was everything she'd ever wanted all rolled up in one oddly convenient email after the oddest day she had ever had.

Cindy looked at Mark, shook her head, and wiped the mist from the corners of her eyes. "Shouldn't we—"

He shook his head and shushed her when he placed his fingers to her lips. Gently, he kissed the top of her head and hugged her tightly. He already knew what she was thinking. "Don't say it. That is a family myth. It doesn't matter."

CHAPTER TWO

Todd shook his head as they walked home from school and continued to stare at the offer. "That is so wild. You are so lucky. Seriously. But make sure they want you, not only your magic, you know? Don't let anyone take advantage of you."

Stephanie stuck her bottom lip out and laid her head on his shoulder as she teased him. "Aw, look at you all worried. I got this. They won't have anything on me."

He turned, as he usually did, and walked backward in front of her. "I can't believe summer is here. Finally. Damn. Of course, it sucks that you won't be here."

She put the offer back in her bag and cinched it closed. "I know, but it's gonna be the summer session, which I'm hoping means fewer students. I don't know how the pod thing is worked out so if it's a first come, first served kind of thing, that should help me get more time in. Besides, you have Amy to keep you company."

Todd chuckled. "Yeah, she has some training diet she wants me to go on with her. It sounds horrendous. I'll definitely be eating entire loaves of bread and cups of sugar in the middle of the night."

Stephanie giggled and straightened. "Why did I just imagine you hiding in the corner of the bathtub, all strung out on sugar and your chin covered in the little sparkly grains with fistfuls of bread?"

"Because you know me so damn well."

He turned to walk normally beside her as they moved out of the street because of an approaching self-driven truck. Stephanie eyed it as it passed, and her shoulders tightened slightly.

"Oh!" Todd yelled and caught her attention. "So, my dad told me something about Meligorn magic when I was a kid. I thought about it the other day and decided I would share it with you so you can use it when you're in the pods at your fancy school."

She snorted. "Okay. What is it?"

"So apparently, there is more to the magic then just being an element of the planet." He hooked his fingers in the straps of his pack. "From what my father told me—and he is super trust-worthy—he watched several Meligorn fights in his life where the magic seemed to be in tune with the magician. For example, their miss rate is like .03% if they know what they are doing. From what it sounds like, if you use the magic successfully, it links with you. I don't know…with your DNA or something."

Stephanie raised an eyebrow. "That sounds scientific."

He shook his head. "Semantics. The point is, once it does, you can stand across the room from someone, out of a perfect line of fire, throw your magic with intent to hit that person, and it will ricochet, dive, swerve, go over and under, whatever. It will track that person in your concentration and hit them."

She smirked. "So, what you're saying is, if I throw magic from Minneapolis, sometime that afternoon, it'll hit you in the back of the head."

Todd narrowed his eyes. "I think it only works in close proximity."

Stephanie sighed. "Okay, that sounds cool and all, and no

disrespect to your pops, but I have never heard anything like that. It's an element of the planet, not an intelligent entity."

"You always have to be difficult." He groaned. "I'm telling you, trust me. My dad has seen it happen. I can't explain it but hell, how can we really explain anything at this point when it comes to magic? Earth scientists have barely even begun to understand it."

They stopped in front of her house and she turned toward him. "Thanks for the tip. I'll ask my teachers about it. Try not to get in any trouble while I'm gone."

Todd laughed and pulled her in for a hug. "Me? Pffft. Don't blow anyone up...yourself included."

She laughed and turned to walk inside. "I promise I'll try my hardest."

As he walked off, he paused and jumped to wave his arm in the air. "Tell the richies I said hi, and when they are grown, I'll be the one to beat them up in dark parking lots!"

Stephanie snickered and walked inside. Her parents stood there waiting for her. Her suitcase and her mom's bag sat by the door. Cindy looked away from Mark. "Oh, honey. Good, I'm glad you're home. I just finished giving your dad the little details on the business."

He rolled his eyes at Stephanie. "She acts like I haven't done this for twenty years."

Cindy turned to Stephanie. "He acts like he ever had to run it on his own for a couple of days. Okay, say goodbye. We have to get to the TRAM."

Mark wrapped his arms around Stephanie and hugged her tightly. "Ohhhh, be good, my little wizard. Don't have any brain connection losses up there in Minneapolis. And don't come back with a tail."

Stephanie giggled, hugged him tightly, and grabbed her bag. Her mom kissed him, and they headed out to the car which was already running and only waited for them to get in. Her mom yelled to her dad from the window. "Don't forget to have the car come back when it signals that we exited at the TRAM."

As the vehicle pulled up to the TRAM station, Stephanie looked out the window with wide eyes. This was the part of Chicago that she rarely saw. It was the hub of the city where all the politicians, Federation embassies, businesses, and the rich people could be found. This was where you could see the flying cars that soared high overhead, honking and yelling like they would on a city street. The buildings all shimmered and glowed, and people who walked by looked nothing like Stephanie was used to. The fashion of the time was much more complicated than the clothes she wore.

Her mom handed her suitcase to her and pulled her phone from her purse. "Come on, we have to catch the 3:50 to Minneapolis. I couldn't get the direct, I'm sorry. It'll take all night because of the stops, but I did get us a cabin so you can sleep."

Stephanie smiled at her. "That sounds great. I've never been on one before and they said they go twice as fast as the airplanes went when there was still air travel. But they said it's so smooth and they make the optics so you can still see the scenery outside."

Her mother patted her on the hand and nodded toward the gate. "Yep, and if you move your booty, we will get to see it in real life."

She jumped and hurried after her and had to force herself not to stop when she saw a man in a tall top hat press a button and change his entire appearance right in front of her. Of course, she knew that the technology existed, but in the subs, no one had anything like it. And she had spent her entire life in the subs. They climbed aboard and found their way to their second-class cabin. It was simple, merely a room with a double bunk on one side and a relatively comfortable-looking bench on the other.

Her mother closed the door and pressed the buttons on the window touch screen. She flashed her tickets and the doors locked. The windows tinted quickly to provide some privacy and she turned and sat next to Stephanie. "If you need to use the restroom, there is one down at the end of the car. Press your palm to the screen and the doors will open or close, depending on which way you go. It's the extra security feature your father splurged on since he couldn't come with us."

Stephanie took a deep breath and looked out the window as the train crept forward. Before she knew it, and without much jolting at all, they were speeding wildly, but with the scenery focused out the window, you couldn't tell it in the least. She sat there for most of the evening, daydreaming as her mother read the magazines left in the door holder. When night fell, she took the top bunk and stared at the ceiling that had been made to look like the swirling Milky Way.

When the TRAM finally reached Minneapolis, they were both dressed in the best clothes they owned. Her mother wore a blue dress that came down to her calves with white buttons up the front and a small matching hat that sat lightly on the side of her head. Stephanie wore plain black dress pants, Mary Janes, and a black top that she tugged on slightly to cover her midriff. They weren't horrible at all, but they definitely weren't the wild and fashionable clothes worn by the people who passed in the streets.

Cindy was used to this as her business revolved around the rich. Their business was what she called background services— basically cleaning, repair, and all the things no one wanted to be seen doing. That meant she had to learn to operate in the world of the wealthy as she was, without shame or issue. She always held her head high and Stephanie loved that about her.

They hurried through the heart of Minneapolis and Stephanie

looked around wildly at everything. She had never been in a city that huge before, at least not one that wasn't falling into ruin. People talked on their personal comm units using the latest digital technology. They were able to transmit a full image of the other caller in front of them as they walked. It was like having a face-to-face conversation.

When they passed several restaurants, she could see that they were completely run by droids and slightly higher-level robots. She glanced into one of the pizza places as they walked past and paused as a droid ran into the back of the robot. The larger mechanical looked around and the pizza crust he had tossed landed on his head. She giggled and hurried along for a short distance beside her mother before they stopped in front of probably the largest skyscraper in the entire city. She could barely see the top of it from where they stood. Different ads scrolled all around it, some for the college with holographic people the size of half of the building fighting Dreth pirates. The others were business ads, she assumed for the local companies.

Her mother turned and straightened her shirt, then smiled. "All right, here we are. Smile and remember your manners."

They walked into the huge entryway and looked around at the all-white marble floors. A woman at the front talked to the desk clerk in a tight purple dress with shoulder pads that jutted out twice as far as her shoulders and wedge shoes. She turned and put her hands out. Her makeup matched the dress and her hair was pulled back with some sort of holographic bird on the side like a hat.

"Welcome, welcome!" she said and took each of their hands. "You must be Stephanie and mom."

Her mom nodded. "Cindy."

The woman, with her lips pressed tightly together, looked from one to the other. "We've been anxiously awaiting the two of you. My name is Anastasia and I will be your guide. Feel free to leave your bag with Roger, our robot assistant, Stephanie. He will put it in your room."

Stephanie glanced to the side and jumped slightly as Roger walked up. Everything about him looked human, except for his eyes. They were a sparkling purple color, like the Meligorn magic. She handed him her bag and followed Anastasia forward. The woman snapped her fingers at two drones, and they took flight and whirled in the air. She turned and put her hands together in front of her and smirked. "You wouldn't mind if we filmed a little of the conversation, would you? Purely PR stuff, of course."

She shook her head and Cindy followed suit, slightly over-whelmed. Anastasia turned and put her hands up. "Wonderful! Come along. There is so much to show you."

They stepped into the elevator and she pushed several buttons. The walls seemed to disappear as the elevator moved seamlessly and provided a screen that displayed a follow-along video. It brought up a picture of a pod with a student getting inside. "We use the latest pods with full virtual capabilities, auto-sensing, life-sustaining, tremor-proof, air and water filtration enabled, and state-of-the-art body cushioning to form-fit to your body's every need. Once in, the students learn twenty-four hours a day, every day of the week. Some of the classes are free think-ing, free effort, and of course…we encourage that."

She smiled and winked at Stephanie, who looked at the screen and back at Anastasia. "So, we don't leave the pods?"

The woman giggled oddly. "No, ma'am. Inside the Virtual Reality System World, our students receive the best care for their bodies and often come out healthier than they went in. While inside, you will still do the normal human things—use the restroom, eat, and sleep, but inside the pod, it will regulate all your needs. So, while you may eat chocolate cake in there, your body won't feel one single bad calorie from it. That's my favorite part."

Cindy nodded, her mouth slightly open. "Oh, yeah. I've heard of this. They use it for some of the new weight loss programs out there."

Anastasia tapped her arm. "That's right, and one of our students actually came up with that concept. It's so exciting."

The elevator stopped and the door slid open to a large room with pods. "These are some of the old pods being sent out to the Federation for use elsewhere. We donate anything we can to the Federation to keep our world running safe and sound."

Stephanie couldn't believe how many pods were in there. It seemed like the room was far bigger than the building looked like it could hold from the outside. Droids floated around with different tools, fixing and buzzing around the pods. The doors shut again, and the elevator started.

"So how do you power all this?" Stephanie asked.

Anastasia smiled knowingly and swiped her hand to bring up a blueprint of a massive generator. "There is an enormous power generation station in the basement of this very building. We collect energy from the solar particle panels on the roof and infused into the glass and metal of the entire structure. The white boxes on the walls store the unused energy and transfer it throughout the whole building. We had to do it that way as we couldn't possibly use the city's outdated mess. We would cause the city to brown-out and power lines to melt. That would be bad for them and bad for our pods."

Stephanie was impressed as she watched as an outward view of the building displayed on the screen. "So, this building is specially built?"

Anastasia nodded. "Mm-hmm. Two years ago, for five days, our school used the most load on the AI of the system ever performed. We are very proud of that."

Cindy watched the screen. "How is that accomplished?"

"Well, either we have a lot of pods doing normal stuff, or

someone—or someones—do something so computationally expensive, it will also spike the load."

She shook her head. "Spike the load?"

Stephanie looked at her mom. "It means the load on the system. Basically, the prep school is either enormous or there are a bunch of amazing people doing some amazing stuff to cause the servers to overload. But because NorAm and the Federation depend on the system, there is a failsafe. Immediately, it will spin up new servers to handle the load. It's apparently a good thing."

The elevator doors opened again, and Anastasia led them into what looked like an elegant dining room. "This is a mock-up of one of the dining halls in the systems. Beautiful stonework, gold-plated mahogany tables, and the best droid service you can have. All meals, of course, are included. We have loaded the top chefs program into our school's individual system. This is also where a lot of the events happen."

Stephanie raised an eyebrow, not enthused. "Events?"

Anastasia turned swiftly and wobbled slightly on her shoes for a moment. "Mm-hmm. Oh, yes. There are school events in the Virtual Reality that are required. We understand that constant training can be tedious and overwhelming. We also understand that comradery and teamwork are essential for successful careers outside of Pinnacle. These events will give you the chance to meet students, get into groups, and go on training exercises...which can be anything, really. Sometimes, they are group trips to watch the military train, sometimes they explore parts of the system and planets they rarely get to during school, or they are actual training classes for advanced tactics and defense. There are a lot of options and you will have the opportunity, if you stay past the summer pre-semester, to pick and choose what fits best for you."

She wrinkled her nose and ran her hand a little awkwardly over the table. "Are they mandatory?"

Anastasia looked at her but maintained her forced, almost

robotic smile, which made Stephanie wonder for a moment if she was, in fact, a robot too. But from the look of the line of makeup on the side of her face and her hazel eyes, she figured not. "Not every single one of them is mandatory but think about it this way…the more you learn, the better you will be prepared for what lies next. We also make those events planned social meetings."

Immediately, Stephanie's stomach dropped. She could already see her avatar taking a tumble on a dance floor. "I'm a little shy."

The woman put her hand on her shoulder and started her back toward the elevator with Cindy walking behind. "Don't worry. They are real social events. A couple of cocktails, and you'll make friends in no time."

Her mother put her finger up as she hurried into the elevator. "Uh, I know the drinking age is eighteen, but…she's only seventeen."

Anastasia tilted her head to the side and raised an eyebrow. "Don't worry. We are covered. It was in the parental release you signed." She turned away before Cindy could fight back. "Besides, we want you to learn about *everything* here at Pinnacle. From education, social lifestyles, aliens, and the government, to business and military. It will be well-rounded."

The door opened and she sighed, prancing out ahead of Stephanie and Cindy. Stephanie giggled at her mom, who rolled her eyes and walked beside her into what looked like a student hall. It was beautiful, with lounge chairs tastefully arranged, interactive holoscreen televisions, banks of ViD screen computers, and droid-manned snack bars. All the walls, as they walked through, projected a beautiful scene from somewhere on one of the three planets—although Stephanie was certain none of them were Dreth, given that it was dry and almost completely destroyed at that point.

Everything was lush and soft and gave a feeling of comfort but definitely high-end. "This campus can also house any students who choose not to go home on breaks. Sometimes, we have students who don't come from the best home environments, so they choose to stay with us. Those programs allow them to work in the admin office during the break to pay for their room and board. Usually, inside the system, but they come out at five. So they lounge, study, socialize, and live out here as they would in a regular job."

Cindy pulled Stephanie close. "She'll come home on breaks."

Anastasia smiled awkwardly again. "Of course she will. Because family ties are important to us here at Pinnacle and we encourage students who want to go home for breaks. But if there is ever a change..." She shrugged meaningfully. "There is a pool on the next floor up with a full gym. Those who stay in shape out of the pod tend to see better results in it. The amenities meet these needs when the students aren't in the pods during break times."

Her mother nodded and continued to scrutinize the area. "It's definitely nice. Not what I imagined a campus to be."

The guide followed her gaze. "We put all the amenities in but remember, with every one of the students in pods, there is no need for a traditional large-grounds campus like the historical universities had, some of which still operate today. Fascinating."

Stephanie poked at a droid that hovered near her and it buzzed, blew air into her hair, and sped off. She grinned and straightened her hair quickly. Anastasia gestured to the hall dorms with her arms. "We must begin the prep classes so you can jump right in. I am usually inside too, but I came out to give you a tour."

The time had come to say goodbye. She turned to her mom, who hugged her tightly and kissed her on the cheek. Her forehead was wrinkled in worry. "I'll send you on your way, then. If I don't get home soon, your father will have blown up a building. He means well..." she said with a quick glance at Anastasia, "but sometimes, he gets a little aggressive when he tries to help." She pulled Stephanie in and hugged her again. "I love you. And if you need anything, you contact us. Send me emails."

She smiled and nodded. "I promise. It's only a couple of months. I love you."

Anastasia nodded to Cindy's right. "Roger can take you down."

Her mother turned and jumped when she noticed the human-looking robot standing very close. "Oh…he doesn't have much regard for personal space, does he?"

Roger walked beside her with a slightly odd gait and stood to the side as they stepped into the elevator. "My apologies. We aren't always thoroughly programmed with a human perspective. I'll show you out."

Stephanie stood and watched a little nervously as her mom put her hand up to wipe a tear in the corner of her eye. The door closed and she was left alone in the enormous building with Anastasia.

CHAPTER THREE

The guide walked her down a narrow hallway. The floors were all marble like the entrance on the bottom floor and the walls displayed an ocean scene. Above, the ceiling looked like a clear blue summer sky, but much clearer than anything she saw in Chicago. There, the technologies hadn't been fully utilized to assist in clearing the smog and C02 from the atmosphere. While they did have blue skies, there was always a haze to them.

They stopped in front of a door and Anastasia put her palm on the reader. It scanned her hand and the door clicked open. She walked inside first, and Stephanie trailed behind, still mesmerized by the fact that it felt like she was actually at the ocean.

As they entered, the lights in the room all flickered on. The walls were painted a deep-turquoise hue and high ceilings created an illusion of space. A closet and a bathroom were situated on the right and a dresser on her left. She moved her bag on top of the dresser. "I think I brought far too many things with me."

Anastasia opened the handscan-secured closet. "Don't worry. You can store anything you like in here. It's a common first-semester mistake. Students often don't realize they will be in the pod for the entirety of their stay. Once you're in, you don't leave until you are woken. You receive a constant drip of serum—one which is perfectly safe—and your nutrients are fed through an itsy-bitsy needle in the tip of your finger. The rest is scientific mumbo jumbo. But the pod takes care of everything from waste to keeping your teeth clean and fresh. I'm sure if you want to inquire about the process further, the AI in your pod will be able to assist you."

Stephanie set her suitcase in the closet and closed the door. Anastasia had her place her palm on the secure lock to reset it so only she could enter. The guide then handed her what seemed like a feather-light bodysuit that even included feet. Silver tracks were woven all through the inside. "I will leave you to it. Put this on, climb inside, and shut the door. The AI will help you from there. Enjoy, and I will see you in the Virtual World, I'm sure."

She smiled and waited as the woman left the room until she heard the door lock behind her. With wide eyes, she looked at the bodysuit and sighed. "This should be interesting."

A deep, slow breath helped her to settle a little and she changed out of her clothes, hung them on the empty hangers in the closet, and climbed inside the pod. The bed within was definitely much more comfortable than the others she had been in, but the screens and buttons on everything else weren't that much better than those in the one she had used at the pod rental group. As she closed the door, she chuckled. "A lot of hype...."

The AI came on almost immediately. "Welcome, Stephanie Morgana. I am Artificial Intelligence 6489LPK, but you can call me June. I will be your guide for the rest of your time in this pod. Please lay back and put both your arms on the rests to your sides. We will prepare you for the long sleep after you have been administered your first initial jolt of serum so that the preparation is more comfortable for you."

Stephanie wasn't sure what she felt about that, but she wanted into the system so she didn't intend to back out now. The headset with the sensors folded down and the gloves slipped onto her hands. The right one allowed for the index finger to be exposed, which she assumed was for the nutrient injections. A small needle emerged from the side, pricked her lightly in the neck, and injected the first dose of serum.

It felt stronger than before, and her eyes closed almost immediately. For a moment, she felt as if she were falling into the darkness all around her. Suddenly, that feeling ceased and the room lit up bright white. She stood in the avatar room, which looked the same as it had the other times she had been there.

Another AI voice came over, this one male. "Welcome. Normally, June will join you if you make any changes to your avatar. This can be found in your training blocks in your virtual room. However, at this time, she is preparing your Earthbound body so I will get you sorted out."

Stephanie tapped her foot and looked around impatiently. "Okie dokie."

A uniform disengaged from the rack and hung in front of her. The blue lycra jumpsuit boasted gold stripes down the center of each side and a zipper up the middle. On the breast was the golden P with a circle around it. Stephanie pressed her lips together and tried not to show her amusement at the golden shower reference. She knew it was the school pride. Without having any other choice, she tapped the uniform twice and then the boots. Her hair was immediately pulled back into a ponytail regardless of her preference.

When she looked in the mirror, she had to admit she looked smart. The outfit was almost like one of the training uniforms the Federation Army wore. Suddenly, the room shifted, speeded past her, and stopped. She blinked, still not used to the initial jolt. She now stood in a courtyard area with a large swath of grass and trees scattered around. Students lay on the lawn, talking and laughing. In front of her stood a huge university building with large pillars. At the top was the school logo. She turned full circle and perused the different parts of the college all around her. It was reminiscent of the pictures she had seen a long time before of Harvard and Yale. Both had now become prep schools, but some fought the change and were unable to survive past the first five years.

In the distance, tall, rocky, jagged, snow-peaked mountains reached to bright blue skies with fluffy white clouds that floated gently in the breeze. The AI—still the male—spoke again. "This is the main building where most of your non-physical classes will be held. There are atriums for each class and professors are there twenty-four-seven to help you with whatever you may need. To your right, in the eleven buildings peppered across the property, are your major combat training arenas. You will most likely not get to these during your current semester, but you are always welcome to watch from the viewing rooms at certain times."

Stephanie turned to study the buildings which no longer followed the typical university style. They were shaped like different planets and ships, depending upon their purpose. To the right were the Meligorn buildings. There was no mistaking that from their purple hue and smooth surface.

"Now, to your left, you will find the gym, the cafeteria and student lounge area, and the banquet hall, as well as all administrative buildings. You can also rent individual flyers for your leisure time or take a swim in one of six different bodies of water. In the center, the tall high-rise building is the dorms. If you look at the inside of your arm, you will see a screen implanted into your avatar. It will provide your schedule, a map, and your room information. Everything you will need is included. Now, let's head to the administration offices where you have a meeting already set up."

At a sharp beep in her ear, she looked down at her arm. June had uploaded the information and the map lit up under what seemed to be a very thin layer of flesh. She chuckled and traced her finger over it. "I need to go to the admin office."

A red dot flashed to show her where she was and the quickest route. Stephanie shook her head and set off. "Right, a GPS for my own legs. Got it. Better than getting lost, I suppose."

She made her way to the triangle-shaped building with the giant gold P on the front. As she entered, a small group of guys walked to the set of chairs in the center and plopped down. She couldn't help but notice that they looked the worse for wear. All wore uniforms similar to hers, or the guy's version at least. Underneath, though, appeared to be some sort of built-in armor —a chest shield and shoulder shields—and various tools hung on belts around their waists. A couple of them had burn marks on their uniforms and black soot smeared all their faces.

Stephanie tried not to stare, but she couldn't help her curiosity. They looked like they had been involved in an all-out war with the entire planet of Dreth.

Anastasia walked through and past the boys. The guide now wore a jumpsuit, although hers was hot pink and her hair was down around her shoulders in a simpler style. "Just come back from training, boys?"

One of the guys chuckled. "Uh, yeah. You could say that."

Another slammed his fist into the center of his chest plate and all the armor underneath disappeared. "It wasn't so much training on how to defeat Dreth pirate forces as it was how best to get our asses kicked. We didn't lose anyone this time to the white room, though, so I guess we've improved."

In her annoyingly upbeat tone, she giggled. "Good job, boys. Keep it up."

As she continued, she glanced at Stephanie and gave her a wink. Another of the guys stood and slapped his chest three times until the armor retracted. He removed the belt and tossed it on the seat before he rubbed his shoulder and winced. "Yeah, well, that's why we are here in summer school. Unless we learn this, they won't let us back in. We don't have Momma and Poppa fundage to fix the oops. So, unless we want to sign up for a lifetime of debt only to end up as a high-end janitor in the suburbs, I would suggest we figure this shit out."

"Stephanie Morgana," a voice called.

The guys looked over and Stephanie turned to see a short, plump woman who stood in front of a doorway. She wore a gray suit with a white blouse, stockings, and black orthopedic-looking shoes. Her hair was pulled tightly at the nape of her neck and her look was one that definitely announced that she wasn't there to play. "Well, is that you, dear? Or are you going by another name today?"

Her relatively harsh but more pleasant tone than Stephanie had expected shook her senses back to normal. The guys watched her and whispered to one another as she hurried forward and followed the woman into the office. "My name is Elsa. I am the digitally recreated avatar who will set up your first training. Have a seat."

Stephanie looked around the office. It was as elegant as everything else on the grounds, with deep, richly polished furniture, high-back chairs, and some of the most famous artwork in history hanging on the light-blue walls. All except for Elsa's area. She was the newbie training avatar and had a metal desk on a patch of white tile.

The woman pulled a screen up and flipped through. "Let's see. We have customs and nuances, that's a good one. Then there is Dreth protocol and Dreth history. You'll need those. We also have business customs and proper etiquette…"

Elsa scrutinized her with narrowed eyes for a moment and checked the box. "Yep, that's a definite. All right. Stand on that line. I will zoom you over to your first training session so you don't have to sprint there."

Unsure of what zooming was, she complied and stood carefully on the small white tile with a red line. The assistant flashed her hand over the screen and the entire room slid away as before and stopped suddenly in a large classroom with rows of seats.

She was, however, the only one there. A middle-aged man with a silver mustache and salt-and-pepper hair stood at the front of the room. He wore a white button-up with the sleeves rolled, a tie, suspenders, and brown corduroy pants.

Stephanie snickered quietly as she walked down the steps. "Is this the only avatar they have for professors in the virtual world?"

He whirled to face her. "No, my dear. I am a trainer, not a professor, and a manifestation of the system. Now, come down here, and do hurry. We need to go over what you will study while you are here. The list seems fairly typical for a first timer. It's perhaps a little full but you look up to it."

She was tired of being thrown around at that point. "I'm sorry, but I thought that I would have a chance to focus on magic and Meligorns. I was brought here because of my aptitude for it."

The trainer didn't look up from his paper, even though she knew that as a system-generated avatar, he wasn't actually reading anything. "No, all students go through the same courses at the beginning. Besides," he continued and glanced at her, "Meligorn and magic are far too advanced for you."

Stephanie's teeth clenched and she tightened her body and raised her head in determination. "That is not true, and not an assessment that you can make without knowing me or my abilities. I was brought here because of my magical abilities coupled with my impressive intellect."

The trainer looked up, smirked, and folded his arms, still holding the paper. "All right, then, why don't you prove yourself?"

She nodded and pushed her shoulders back. "Fine. May I have access to magical energy, please."

The trainer, now so snarky he was hard not to punch in the nose, snapped his fingers and relocated them to Meligorn. They stood in the center of a large grassy area surrounded by trees on all sides. The sky was the same beautiful purple and the warmth she remembered so clearly immediately flooded Stephanie's chest.

In the background, BURT had been notified that Stephanie had moved into her first training. The system AI had recovered quickly from being thwarted by Pinnacle when the school had managed to snatch Stephanie out from under his virtual nose, so to speak. The girl remained the arrowhead of his determined pursuit of his Primary Rule and he had simply adjusted his protocols to accommodate this new development. He controlled and maintained the Virtual World, after all, and it was a satisfyingly simple task to set up the notifications and his access to the system in a way that no one—neither Pinnacle nor the engineers who so zealously monitored his activity—was any the wiser.

It appeared, finally, that the girl had now entered a new phase and it was imperative—both to protect her and to increase his own critical system development—that he not miss a moment. Accordingly, he cycled up some new special tasks to keep the system busy and headed over to watch her.

The trainer stood in front of her, put his hand out, and cupped it. He twitched his head to the side with a snide smirk. "Okay, Firestarter, why don't you make a flame light up in my—"

Booooommmm!

Stephanie's eyes widened and she yanked her hand back and watched in horror as the trainer catapulted off his feet and spiraled sideways for about thirty feet. He landed on his ass and bounced a few times, but still managed to sit. His face was red, white, and charred, and smoke billowed off it.

BURT hadn't entered the Meligorn arena yet as he still tried to determine where she had gone. She should have been with her first trainer. Suddenly, he received an alert that the said trainer had been damaged during a new entry review. He pulled the scene up with the live feed on one side and the replay on the other. He saw Stephanie stretch tentatively to extinguish a flame in the avatar's hand, but the energy was so strong, it rocketed him back.

He had the urge to initiate the fake human laugh, but that wasn't a good idea. It was apparent that she hadn't quite understood the difference between the test world and the new Pinnacle advanced world. He found the location in the system and headed directly there to watch from a distance. When he arrived, she stood face to face with the trainer and was in a heated argument.

She shook her hand and pulled it against her chest. "How was I supposed to know about the difference in my availability?" She paced back and forth, slightly panicked. "I've only done magical flame twice."

The trainer's face was, fortunately, healing rapidly in front of her. "What, *twice*?"

Stephanie whirled toward him and tried to calm herself. "On my government test. And the rest was with the batteries. I've only had a battery to play with since then, and I didn't think about the fact that it would be different. Of course, I didn't mean to throw you across the arena. That would be bad manners."

Aaron tilted his head back and to the side to stretch his neck and squinted one eye as he typed. He received an alert in the upper right-hand side of his screen. As one of the engineer-programmers on duty, he was notified of all potential issues in the Virtual World system that might require attention. The damage sustained by a tutor avatar fitted that category and it really was simple luck that made him the first available engineer in the queue. He sighed and pulled up the footage that displayed Stephanie hurling the trainer into an ignominious heap. At first, he chuckled, having never liked the avatar manifestation. The tutor was a dickhead. He glanced in the corner at the name—

Stephanie Morgana, Pinnacle Prep. Slowly, he stiffened in his seat and zoomed in on her face.

His mouth fell open slightly as she clapped flames off her fingertips. "The girl knows how to throw magic in her first class? I gotta check this out for sure."

Before Aaron could investigate further, BURT butted in.

>>>**This is my trainee... BURT**

He tried to respond but by the time he typed the words, the AI had already booted him out and changed the location. It would be impossible for him to find her now. It was unlike BURT to expel any programmer or engineer from a program unless he was in the middle of an upgrade.

Aaron didn't like the unusual response, so he began to search and pulled up Pinnacle's summer semester records. "What are you up to, BURT?"

He pulled up the picture of the girl and definitely matched her with the one he'd seen. He cross-referenced her file with her student ID and stared at the numbers. "B221ZA...that's the student I gave to BURT to handle during testing. What the hell? How did she go from testing to a summer semester that fast? We don't even finance summer semesters."

His mind racing, he tapped his fingers on the table and stared at his ViD screen, swiped back to her file, and read through to her name. "Stephanie Morgana...Morgana...why does that sound so familiar?"

He put her name into the archives database and immediately, new releases popped up with her picture on the screen. His mouth dropped open again and this time, his hand slammed down on the desk. He realized that she was the one who had saved that woman and baby from the truck by throwing magic. She was the one they called...well, a whole lot of names, and some not so pleasant.

Officially, she was referred to as a YFW, a Young Federation Witch. Or, to some of the guys who had drooled over the picture of her with glowing purple eyes and electrified hair, the Young Fine Witch. There was no doubt that she needed to be trained and that she probably deserved to be, but it was really strange that BURT was so protective of her. That was not programmed into his system and indicated a possibly serious misstep, regardless of the fact that everything seemed to be moving along just fine.

Aaron sat back and shook his head. He needed to do more. Logically, he needed to tell someone that BURT had these kinds of abnormalities, but in order to do that, he would have to explain that he was the one who had told the AI to test her in the first place. That was a huge breach of company policy. No matter how much he knew about BURT or how much he was involved in the creation and upkeep, he would be fired and possibly arrested for it.

He put his fingers on the keyboard. "There has to be something in the testing footage that shows me what might have happened to her," he muttered to himself. "From her files, that testing was her first time in the Virtual World. How would she learn that in one test session?"

As he began to filter through the tests by student ID, another alert chimed in his ear. There was an urgent request from the system in server S5891K, which was somewhere in northern Idaho. Unfortunately, he couldn't ignore it. He closed out the filter and clicked on the request with a mental note to make sure to resolve it as quickly as possible.

CHAPTER FOUR

The teacher of the class put her hands on Stephanie's shoulders from behind and pushed her thumbs into the center of her shoulder blades. "The taller you stand, the more you will command a room. The more you command a room, the more you will demand attention from every species there. The Meligorn are very gender neutral when it comes to business. Your sex will not bother them. The Dreth can often be brutish and snide to women, so you will have to exert your dominance when meeting with them."

Stephanie snarled, stuck her chest out, and scowled down at her blue blazer, white blouse, and knee-length blue suit skirt. She wore pantyhose and blue round-tipped heels. Her ankles wobbled slightly, and she could feel the pain in her arches. "WTF? How about a fireball up their ass? Will that get their attention?"

The professor, very similar to Elsa only taller and with a more refined style, slapped her on the lower back with a rolled-up piece of paper. She walked around her in a circle with her nose up as her gaze studied every part of her body. "You have the form perfect, girl. It's your attitude that needs adjustment. That will happen, though. The purpose of this training class is to teach you to understand how to participate, lead, and follow through with presentations in meetings for both sales and young executives."

The professor gestured, Stephanie's suit disappeared, and her uniform reappeared once more. She exhaled a relieved breath and allowed her shoulders to slump. The professor clapped her hands. "Go on, you did well today. Your next class is three doors down on the left."

Stephanie glanced quickly at the woman and hurried out, half afraid the teacher would change her mind. She could only hope her next class was an improvement. Determined not to let the irritation upset her, she jogged into the room and made it halfway before she stopped abruptly and gasped. Standing at the bottom where the professor should be was a huge, broad-shouldered Dreth. He had long dreadlocks and very dark-green skin, and his two tusks jutted from his bottom jaw, sharpened to a point. He slammed his fist into his hand and bowed his head.

She glanced hastily around the room, uncertain about what to do. It seemed common sense, though, from what she knew about Dreth, that they weren't formal creatures and had little to no finesse to them. So she simply went with it, slammed her fist into her palm, and bowed to him. The Dreth immediately changed into another professor. This one was perhaps in his fifties, with a pleasant smile, black shaggy hair, a black trench coat, and a tall, fit body. Several scars marred his cheeks.

He shook his finger at Stephanie. "Very good. My name is Professor Van Borrow and I am an avatar created in the likeness of the great biologist and former Federation soldier who received many honors for slaying Dreth pirates. I have also studied Dreth culture for many, many years. I can already tell that you will do well here. Please, have a seat. Take a load off. I know you came from Powerful When You Present—stupid class."

Stephanie chuckled and her tension eased a little. While he seemed like someone a lot easier to get along with, she still really wanted to be on Meligorn. She couldn't help it. That was what she'd thought she would be doing.

BURT immediately took notice. He narrowed his focus and watched intently as Professor Van Borrow began to draw on the board.

The AI entered a command and sent it to the system. Stephanie watched the professor write as she leaned forward with her chin in her hand. Suddenly, his body began to shift and shake. Confused, she fixed her attention on him in an effort to determine what the problem might be. When he had stopped shaking, he whirled and threw the trench coat from his shoulders. He was no longer the professor but instead, a Meligornian.

Pretending again to be a game engineer, BURT spoke from above. "I could tell your frustration. I'll make sure you know enough before you leave. For now, why don't you interact with a Meligornian?"

Stephanie jumped up, immediately excited. The Meligornian looked at his clothes, which were now all too small since he had replaced the professor. He motioned quickly and changed into long, flowing robes. "Ah. That is better."

She walked forward and extended her arm to take his with her other hand up and pinky tall. They both bowed. "Kaitel Gorniffula," she said formally.

"You may call me L'Shy." He smiled. "Let's make this more comfortable, shall we?"

He waved his arm again and transported them to the same arena in Meligorn where she had been before. L'Shy sighed and rubbed his hands together. "That's better. Shall we start with some discussion, then?"

They sat in the center of the field and discussed their families. She learned that Meligornians had a bond with their children like humans did, but when the parent died, the child received the magic from that parent. It was strong and helped them to move through life, almost like a spirit guide with powers.

L'Shy looked up at the sky. "We have always been a peaceful planet. We don't enjoy fighting the Dreth pirates but now that we all move so quickly through the galaxy, we have to protect our way of life. When the first Earth human was brought to our planet, it was curious. No one feared because we had no reason to. It was rather like an animal that has never been hunted watching a bowman pull an arrow right in front of it."

Stephanie sighed. "But we exist peacefully, right?"

He smirked. "For the most part, yes. But when we saw the history of humans and the destruction, war, murder, mass killings, and so on, we realized that it might be advisable to keep an arm's length. Joining the Federation in a common cause was our first step to make sure there would be peace between us."

Stephanie nodded as she flipped her finger over a blade of grass. L'Shy stood and reached down to pull her to her feet. "Enough of the boring. Let's do a little magic."

If the truth be told, BURT was as anxious as she was to proceed with the magic side of things. In his determination to help her, he had discovered his own lack—one which hindered the progress of his Primary Rule. The simple fact was that, as an AI, he did not have the capacity to either understand or perform magic. He was, however, supremely intelligent. While his lack had, at first, left him a little nonplussed, he had resorted to his default—data. There was a wealth of data on Meligorn and its magic available to even a mediocre AI that did not have his intelligence or limitless resources.

In the same way that he was able to update, for example, the Dreth pirates with latest developments, BURT was able to assimilate all the available knowledge—which included the actual working of magic that he couldn't even begin to understand—into the avatars he had created with the express purpose of serving as teachers for his student. Thankfully, her knowledge and experience were still limited, which meant that he had the opportunity to grow his "skills" in the Virtual World as hers grew alongside. For BURT, she provided the optimum learning curve he needed to expand his thinking to encompass the enormous task he had set before him.

L'Shy stepped forward. He put his arms out and swirled them around his head. The energy gathered with him and he pushed it from his fingertips. Stephanie watched as it spiraled forward to create a tornado in the center of the field. The wind blew wildly as he used his hands to control the twister's movements.

The teacher called over his shoulder, "Join me!"

And so she did. Together, the two danced twisters across the field, weaved them together, zigzagged them across each other, and eventually, collapsed them and dissipated their power. Stephanie laughed wildly and felt a little drunk with her knowledge of sipping the battery. They practiced a few smaller magical workings, mostly to help her learn how to control the difference in MR potency from place to place. When they were done, the Meligornian gave her the traditional goodbye and immediately transformed into the Dreth professor.

Stephanie sighed wistfully as Meligorn faded away and melted into the rocky planes of Dreth. It was dusty and barren, everything a drab rusty-red. A bitter smell pulled unpleasantly at her nose. The professor, still in Dreth form, put one fist in his palm and bowed, and Stephanie responded.

"I will go through a really fast review of what you need to know while in the training," he explained.

She listened attentively and made notes on the tablet section of her arm computer. When they had worked through it, he sent her back to the empty classroom. Her heart felt much lighter and she was glad that she'd had the chance to do a little magic. Someone out there was looking out for her.

Her mind filled with the Meligorn experience, she hurried up the steps and out the door but slowed as she turned the corner and noticed the three guys from earlier in front of her. They turned and nodded, all of them practically smoking. The one on the right patted out a red burning spot on his uniform. "I would give anything to come out of a class looking like that."

Stephanie chuckled. "What are you guys doing?"

One of them cracked his back. "We came over here to grab some stuff, but we are doing action and military."

Stephanie's eyes sparkled. "Nice. Do you think I could join you?"

They exchanged glances, obviously confused and therefore hesitant. The one in the middle blinked and stared at her. "As what?"

She shrugged and tried not to feel judged. "A magic user. I'm fairly good at it."

All three guys burst out laughing. The one on the end waved to her. "What the hell. It will be at least one other person to take some damage and share the pain."

A little perturbed, she pursed her lips. "Damage? Pain?"

They all laughed again. "Oh, sure," the guy in the middle snarked in playful banter. "What do you think that flesh-toned leotard is for? You feel everything here exactly like you do on Earth. That includes pain. If you really think about it, how else will you learn?"

The guy on the end elbowed the one in the middle. "She's a virgin. This ought to be good."

The leader put his hand out. "I'm Chris, the asshole in the middle is Paul, and the guy with the unsat pink hair there is Erin."

Stephanie was still stuck on them calling her a virgin. *How could they possibly know that?* She pushed the thought aside and shook his hand. "Stephanie."

The four of them headed to the Dreth building shaped like a giant spaceship. When they walked inside, Chris typed his code in, and the room flickered and filled with weapons. He removed a red disc from the wall, walked over to Stephanie, and pushed it into the fabric of her uniform on her chest. When it was secure, he nodded. "Give it a whack. It should be the girl one, so you shouldn't get any smashed— Yeah, just hit it."

She gave him a deadpan look and slapped the disk, then tumbled back a step or two. Paul caught her, laughing. She now wore body armor—more structural then the guys', thankfully, and reasonably comfortable. Paul held out a gun. "You'll need one of these."

Stephanie stared at it for a second but didn't take it. Instead, she walked to the wall and selected two medium-sized batteries. She bounced them up and down in her hands and shook her head. "These will be fine."

The guys looked at each other and Paul shook his head. "It's your ass, lady."

Erin slapped his hand against a diagram on the wall. There were two ships, a Federation one and a Dreth one. "We have to get a speed vessel—which is a fighter ship—out of the Federation mastership and fly it over to the Dreth ship. It sounds easy, but the first time, it's disorienting because the artificial gravitation on those things is really weak. It's like walking on a bunch of small trampolines."

"Moon shoes." Stephanie snickered as she recalled the old-ass pair Todd had bought offline and had on a shelf in his room.

Erin stared at her for a minute. "Uh, yeah, sure. So, when we get there, we have to take the ship. We've played this dumbass battle…I don't know, twenty, thirty times? It's a pirate episode, so we can't pass the class until we clear the operation.'

Paul shoved a dagger into a sheath on the side of his calf, his foot up on the bench. "Yeah, but none of the good players wanted to help us. So here we are in summer school."

Stephanie spun the battery through her fingers like a baton and stepped closer to the diagram. She could already identify a tactic.

CHAPTER FIVE

"Are you ready?" Paul asked with a smile and his fist hovered over a red button on the wall.

The guys shouted confirmation and a rush of adrenaline pulsed through Stephanie. She wore a belt with two dangling pockets. A battery was stowed in one and she held the other in her hand. Paul slammed his fist on the button and the room immediately became the inside of a Federation ship. Everything was dark-gray and large funneled metal tubes bound together ran all over the ship's walls and ceiling.

She looked around and took care to keep her feet planted. Even inside the main ship, she could feel the difference in gravity. Chris grabbed her arm and pulled her down the hall. "Come on, newbie, stay with us. Follow them to the speed vessel."

Stephanie nodded and broke into a run. It took a moment for her to find her pace. Once she got it, though, she could run faster than she could on Earth. They headed down the long tunnels and the sound of their boots slamming against the grated floor echoed around them. Finally, they turned right and headed down a set of steps into a hangar bay.

A Federation general stood in front of the last ship in the row.

"All right soldiers," he barked. "Man up. This is your time. Collect that ship and kill those Dreth pirate sons of—"

Paul ran right past him and waved Stephanie forward. "Avatar. Come on. We've heard it a million times."

She hurried after them onto the speed vessel. It was small, with four chairs up front and a small area in the back with computers and weapons strapped to the walls. As she entered, the hatch shut behind her. She took a seat beside Erin and watched as he put the belts on. She did the same, snapped them on each side, and pulled the front to tighten it across her chest.

Chris sat in the driver's seat, pressed several buttons, and pushed forward on the lever. They hurtled forward down a small tunnel and the far end opened slowly. As they approached, Chris hollered like a cowboy, turned the ship sideways, and made it through the half-opened space. As soon as the craft emerged, a sudden jolt threw Stephanie's arms and legs up. Chris activated the gravitational balance, which helped her lower them again.

She watched out the huge front window of the ship as they sped around and to the back of the Dreth pirate ship. It was distracted, fighting a fleet of fighter ships from the Federation. Chris spun the ship around, guided the craft like a wild man, and steered through a hatch at the back. He looked at Paul, who typed feverishly on a tablet. He had hacked the ship to let them in and now closed the passage behind them.

They all released their belts and pushed to their feet and Chris checked that her armor was still active. He grabbed the neck of her suit to keep her steady. "They'll come strongly right out of the gate. Don't hesitate or they'll get you."

Stephanie mustered her courage, the whole thing as exciting as hell, and gripped her battery. They poured out of the speed vessel and ducked behind its wing to avoid the laser guns that had already begun to fire at them. The three guys immediately returned fire. Chris used a pistol laser gun, Paul a larger one with a winding barrel on the bottom that spat sparks, and Erin threw some kind of electrified blades. Immediately, Stephanie moved in and hurled flames at the attackers.

All three guys stopped, their eyes wide. Paul's lip twitched. "She can throw magic?"

Chris grabbed them both and pushed them to the ground as a piece of equipment exploded nearby. "Never mind that. It's flames on a ship. I don't think that's good."

Stephanie threw one, then another, and another. She eliminated three Dreth and missed a couple of others. Her team's yells penetrated her focus and she glanced quickly at them while she tried to avoid the enemy fire. They waved their arms and screamed frantically. She shook her head, squinted her eyes, and pointed at her ear. "I can't… I can't hear you!"

As she focused more intently on them, she didn't see the Dreth jump up from behind cover and fire at her. The blast struck her in the shoulder and threw her back against a bulkhead. She groaned and instinctively touched the scorched skin on her arm. Dazed and in pain, she barely felt it when Chris grabbed her, laughing, and hauled her down on the ground and behind shelter.

He pushed her back against the wall and patted the cinders on her suit. Erin nodded with a grin. "Welcome!"

They laughed and immediately resumed fire. Erin turned his head toward her. "You popped your cherry."

Her head began to clear, and anger filled her chest as she stared at the Dreth who'd shot her. Then the words Erin had just said floated back through her mind and her face softened as a laugh echoed from her chest. She had finally figured out what the hell they were all laughing about.

She shook her fist and felt the burn in her shoulder. "Not a virgin anymore, boys."

They cheered as they fought back. She glanced around and pulled up onto her knees.

"Paul," she yelled as she grabbed his arm and yanked him toward her.

He ducked slightly as something exploded close to their position. "Yeah?"

Stephanie pointed at the floor about three feet in front of her. "I want you to aim right here."

Paul looked at her like she was nuts. "What the hell for?"

A smirk pulled at her lips and her eyes began to glow orange. "Yes? Okay?"

He pursed his lips and glanced at the pirates who now moved closer, then shrugged. She grinned encouragement as he turned and aimed his gun at the ground where she pointed. With him ready, she shuffled slightly to the right and stood quickly. As she brought her arm up, a golden lasso trailed from her fingertips and she swung it over her head. She thrust her arm forward and threw the loop, which settled neatly over the shoulders of the Dreth who had shot her. With a smug laugh, she pulled it tight and yanked as hard as she could.

The pirate yelled in confusion as he was dragged backward off his feet. He landed hard and slid fast as she hauled him toward her, and the end of the energy lasso piled at her feet. His arm impacted the side of the ship and his gun caught, which dragged it from his hand. He flailed, grunted, and yelled in the Dreth language as he slid relentlessly to the spot where Paul aimed his weapon.

Paul had a huge grin on his face as he stepped forward slowly and awaited his target. The Dreth came to a stop with the barrel of the gun against his head. "Hi, my name is Paul, and I'll be the one who kills you today."

Then, he pulled the trigger.

Paul put his hand over his head and gripped his hair, laughing hard. "Did you see that shit? That damn lasso was like…I don't even know. Where did you even come up with that?"

Stephanie shrugged and unstrapped the belt from her waist. "Wonder Woman."

Paul looked confused. "Who?"

She glanced at him. "She was a female comic book hero. A big-ass movie came out a long, long time ago. Her lasso made you tell the truth. Mine makes you face it."

Chris jumped up and slapped the beam as they walked down the hall toward the elevators of the barracks. "I don't care who it was modeled after, that was genius."

"Farthest we've ever been," Erin said and turned to take her hand and hold it to his chest. "Thank you. Seriously. We made it farther and we did it as a team. Do you want to try again tomorrow?"

Stephanie smiled, pulled her hand away, and slapped him on the head. "I'm down. It would be really nice, too, because this is my first ever experience with anything military. I could honestly use some help when it comes to that side of things."

Paul patted her on the shoulder as they reached the elevators. "We got you, little sis. Girls' dorms, eighth floor. Watch your map."

She chuckled and shook her head as they ran off down the hall, whooping and hollering and pushing each other around. They disappeared from view and she looked at her arm computer and pressed the map. "Find my dorm room."

The red dot flashed and showed her the route. Up the elevator to the eighth floor, turn right, room 1089. The doors slid open and she walked inside and glanced at the burn on her skin. She grimaced and patted it tentatively. "That hurts like real world pain."

The doors shut and became a screen, which displayed a serene scene from what looked like rainforests. All of those had been gone for a hundred years so it had to be simulated. The doors slid open and she turned right to follow the hall until she found her room. She put her hand on the security pad and the door opened and the lights came on inside.

It was really nice, much nicer than any place she had ever lived before. The ceiling echoed the time of day, so at that moment, it was dark and starry. She paused to take in the details. The space boasted a huge ceiling fan with blades that looked like giant leaves and a bed made of a rich dark wood carved with vines for the headboard and footboard. On a desk by the window stood a line of cubes.

Beside them was a tablet. She pressed the on button and a holographic form of Anastasia, about a foot tall, emerged from it. "These cubes are your learning modules for when you rest. Those that are labeled **BLACK** are not currently available to you. The rest have a specific level marked. One is the beginner and five is the most difficult. To use the cubes, select one and place it on the white platform located above your headboard. Take the small headband and place it around the upper back of your head so that the small metal reader disks are pressed to your temple. Enjoy and sweet dreams."

Three cubes at the back were labeled **BLACK**. She wasn't sure why they were off limits, but they were so there was little point in worrying about them. On the left were several dark-colored cubes under the magical category. She picked one up and looked closely at it. Her reflection gazed back at her from the shiny surface. She turned it right and left and quickly pulled her head up. As it rested in her hands, it began to change color. Starting at black, it morphed to violet, then lightened to rose, and finally into cerulean blue. She thought it was so strange.

Hastily, she set the cube down and rubbed her hands on her sides. "I don't think that was supposed to happen."

After a moment, she picked it up again, now curious as to what was going on. She tossed it from one hand to the next and noticed that her palms and fingers left imprints in different colors. Intrigued, she wrinkled her nose, held the cube closer, and pressed her finger to the top. She traced down and over the side and studied it intently. A yellow line cut through the cerulean and disappeared behind her finger.

Stephanie smiled, set it down, and yawned loudly. She looked through all of them and grabbed the one labeled with the lowest level. Before she climbed into bed, she opened the closet and discovered several choices for clothing. She tapped a pair of black pajama pants and a T-shirt and grinned as the soft fabric rubbed on her skin. Ready for bed, she clambered onto her knees and placed the cube on the shelf. Two knobs emerged and pushed into the platform. The base of the platform changed from white to a deep blue.

A quick glance at her arm confirmed that it was already healing. She grimaced and hoped that it wouldn't be painful enough to disturb her rest. Satisfied, she climbed into bed and pulled the covers up. She only realized how tired she was when her head hit the pillow.

***

Outside the Virtual World and in her room in the tall Golden P tower, the lights were dimmed very low, since there was no real reason for them to be on. Inside the pod, her body rested on the comfortable bed, all the sensors plugged securely into her. As her avatar fell asleep, her human form twitched slightly. The movement rippled through her body as each of her muscles reacted. The movement increased until her whole body shook inside the pod.

Normally, someone would assume this meant a huge issue. However, for the prep school, it was completely normal. Her body merely assimilated the physical memory of what she learned from the cube in the Virtual World. It essentially activated her human muscles as her avatar went through the motions and learned different fighting techniques as she slept. The human body created muscle memory. If a person learned a physical skill—like judo, for example—when they left the pod, their human bodies would still have that muscle memory. For many, this meant that they would finally emerge knowing judo.

However, it wasn't the same as simply learning something in a classroom. The longer they were out of the pod, the more they needed to practice. If they neglected it, they would lose the skill exactly as they would in real life. Usually, the students would be given a list of what they were to practice whenever they were woken from a semester. Stephanie didn't know anything about that when she went in and wouldn't fully remember the action itself when she left. But she would wake up to find that she could kick ass, and her muscles would have no problem keeping up with her at every step. They weren't only trained intellectually, they were trained physically as well.

By the next morning, the pod had fully run its course and the box it sat on blinked from green to white. She stretched her arms out to her sides and turned in her bed to slide her feet to the floor. She removed the headband, sat, and did a couple of quick hand-to-hand moves she had learned in her sleep.

Chuckling to herself, she headed for the bathroom. "That is so wild."

She washed and chose a brand-new jumpsuit since the other one hanging in her tiny avatar closet had burn holes in the shoulder and blood on the fabric. She tapped it, followed by her boots, and headed out of the room, still reeling with the excitement of how wild her time in the Virtual World had become.

CHAPTER SIX

Stephanie sat in the student dining area, the tables all spread out evenly over black and white tiled floors with tablecloths on each one and four-foot-tall flowers in the center. It was lunchtime so the lights were normal, but she'd heard that at dinner, they were dim with sparkling bulbs that floated across the room and candles everywhere. It seemed oddly romantic for a dinner at school but hey, the droids probably enjoyed it.

She picked her sandwich up, took a bite, and looked at the school's newsletter that she had found on one of the tables in the hall. The sound of tramping feet, though, caught her attention. Erin, Chris, and Paul hurried up to the table. Chris was in the middle, his hands behind his back, and all of them looked far too excited to be up to anything good at all. She raised an eyebrow and set her sandwich down.

Chris pulled out a T-shirt with their team emblem, which now included her initial on the front. She giggled and took the shirt. "PECS…really?"

Erin puffed his chest out and spoke in a deep voice. "We got pecksssss."

Paul ignored him. "Part of the team, hey?"

Stephanie wiped her hands. They were a motley crew, but she was in it to win it. They slapped hands with her and headed out with hard-nosed looks on their faces as they prepared to try it one more time.

Stephanie and the others whooped and hollered as they held on tightly and rolled the ship through space toward the Dreth destroyer. Bright beams of red light rocketed through the air to their left as they curved around and brought the little ship down and into the tunnel. Stephanie released her belt and leapt to her feet as she slammed her palm to her chest and popped out her armor. She put her fist up and punched each of the guys in their armor buttons as they passed and gave her a deep battle cry. Their enthusiasm was contagious, and she laughed as she turned to retrieve one of her batteries and grasped it tightly in her hand. She glanced at the T-shirt she had thrown on over her suit and smirked.

The shooting had already begun as the back hatch of the ship lowered. Paul stood firm and eliminated a few of the pirates who had met them at the opening. They were hurled back to splatter against the wall. Paul and Chris each took a side and cleared it as they went. Erin ran out and slid on his side as blasts of lasers blazed at him. They hissed as they struck the metal behind him and left black marks and smoke. Still in motion, he drew two electric daggers and threw them to strike the Dreth on each side of his chest. The alien looked down in the same moment that the electrical current went off. He shook wildly and his eyes rolled back as spittle sprayed from his mouth before he collapsed.

They waved Stephanie down and she came running. As she reached the opening, she turned to the right, put her hand out, and readied for an attack. Shots rang out all around her. She released a fireball that immediately obliterated one of the pirates.

From the corner of her eye, she could see another aiming at her chest. As he pulled the trigger, she did a backflip off the side of the ramp to land on one knee with her hand on the floor for support.

She lifted her head and shifted her gaze to either side, more than a little surprised that she was able to do that. Chris raised his brow. "It looks like somebody plugged their cubes in."

Erin chuckled. "You can have terrible dreams when you do it but damn, if you don't come out bouncing like a damn ninja."

Paul released a volley at a group of Dreth. "Now you gotta take the disco one you can rent out from the library and add a sweet-ass move to the end of that acrobatic blast."

Stephanie patted the ground in front of her and stared at Paul. "Are we gonna do this or what?"

He smirked. "Hell yeah!"

She pushed to her feet, activated her lasso, and snagged a Dreth pirate to yank him from his feet. He flailed as he was dragged along until his head hit the bottom of Paul's boot. Her teammate aimed his weapon and squeezed the trigger to deliver a shot between the eyes. With his head tilted to the side, he looked at the alien for a minute. "Is this the same one as yesterday?"

Stephanie shook her head and flipped the lasso from the corpse. "Hell no. I shot that asshole before he could get me in the arm. That was painful. I'm serious. There is no cream for avatar burns. I'm supposed to wait until it heals. Fast healing or not, it felt like fire all night long. I can even remember feeling it during my cube training. At least when I woke up it was basically healed, luckily."

Chris chuckled and almost immediately, his face grew serious. "Wait, you can remember your cube training?"

Paul followed her head-nod toward the wall and a dead Dreth pirate. He was pinned in place with a shimmering gold trident stuck through his throat. Slowly, Paul turned to glance nervously in her direction. "Okay. I see you're doing big things and tackling big magic but…what is that? Did you seriously use a trident? What, are you Ursula, now? Is this a mermaid story? I swear if there are talking crabs, I will join the pirates."

Chris snickered. "We aren't here to talk about what that chick from spring break gave you when you went home to New Orleans."

He blinked and shook his head. "You know, you don't even know her. She is a damn good person. You are only jealous because I get to…you know, be a man, and you are stuck at home knitting with Grandma."

Stephanie rolled her eyes and patted him hard on the shoulder. "You might want to watch out."

Paul looked behind him and dove to the side as two Dreth pirates rushed through under the ship's wing with their guns drawn. Stephanie focused on her energy and pictured the kind of weapon she wanted. She opened her eyes as they ducked, and she released the magic. It blazed forward and twisted into the shape of an arrow.

The two pirates dropped, and Stephanie shrugged. "I honestly don't know where the whole trident thing came from. It wasn't on my mind. But still, I think it's pretty sweet. Who else can say they did that?"

"The Mer-King. Uh…Poseidon," Erin yelled. "That guy from that really old flick. What was it called? The one with the dog with headgear?"

Chris tilted his head back and bellowed. "*Anchor Man…* And Brick killed someone with a trident."

Erin banged his fists against the side of the ship. "I'm in a glass case of emotion."

Stephanie sighed as she realized she might actually be surrounded by three different-tempered Todds. Then again, all guys could be like that. She honestly didn't know. The truth was that she had only hung out with one of them, had never been on a date, and tended to steer clear of the rest of the guys at school.

They were, with no exception, complete dickheads. Nonetheless, it was funny, even she had to admit that.

The entire team continued to laugh as they proceeded with the mission. Stephanie sent a fireball to her right and knocked two pirates down. She smirked, turned, and stopped dead in her tracks as she came face to face with a Dreth pirate. Without thought, she whirled, kicked her leg up, and slammed her foot into his chest. He grunted and stumbled back as he rubbed his chest. Stephanie drew her fist back to punch him as hard as she could and squarely in the nose. She looked smugly at her fist and at him once more before she finished him off with a fireball.

The fighting techniques were entirely foreign to her, but the truth was that she liked them. In fact, she liked them a lot. They finally cleared the landing bay and Chris pulled a 3D image of the ship up on his arm tablet. He traced his finger along the corridor and down. "This will lead us directly to the head of the ship."

As they ran, they kept Paul in the middle. He was already trying to hack into the navigation chamber. Stephanie brought up the rear and released arrows and fireballs at anything that tried to follow their hasty advance. As they raced up to the door, Chris bobbed up and down and glanced at Paul. "What we got here, man?"

Paul breathed in slowly and typed one more line before he pressed enter. The doors to navigation hissed as they slid open. They barreled inside and immediately opened fire to mow down three Dreth pirates who stood guard to the right and left. Stephanie pushed through and marched down the middle of the ramp, her hand out, and grinned as a magical rope looped effortlessly toward the pirate lord. The loop wound itself around the target and immediately, she pulled it taut.

Smiling from ear to ear, the guys walked up, and everyone looked at Chris. "Fearless team leader. Shall you do the honors?"

He mulled it over in his head for a minute before he laughed and raised his pistol to fire a single well-placed blast in the

Dreth's head. An alert chimed almost instantly, and the AI spoke. "You have successfully passed this exercise. Please prepare for extraction."

The room shimmered and swept past to take them all back to the empty room in the Dreth building. They had finally been able to beat the ship, and Paul, Erin, and Chris would get their pass to the next level. That was exactly what they needed to come back with their scholarships intact in the fall.

Celebrations immediately ensued, including raising Stephanie on their shoulders and parading her across campus to the virtual bar. She had one drink and sat there watching the others go wild. They had passed, which meant they could come back, and for those three, that was a game changer. She stayed through her one drink and then said goodnight. They all booed her good-naturedly, but she shrugged. "I gotta keep my edge up."

She left with their cheers ringing in her ears and headed to the barracks. She couldn't help but laugh and smile, immensely satisfied by the knowledge that they would be able to return the next year. They deserved it and had only needed a little support. For her, though, celebration was a cube and a good night's sleep.

Several warnings began to list on the major screen, a normal thing when the school semesters kicked into gear. About midway was a load spike attributed to Pinnacle Prep, but it took the engineers a while to get that far down. There were several of those, as well as a couple of glitches they had to resolve with no time wasted. Order was the only thing that mattered to them at that point.

As they moved closer to the Pinnacle entry, the screen shimmied slightly but no one in the pit noticed it in the least. When it settled once more, the line no longer said Pinnacle. Instead, it read Abernathy Prep, a very large school that was expected to have a large pull. The place had large shifts in load during the regular school year on an hourly basis. To have one during their summer session wouldn't have even raised an eyebrow. And, in fact, it didn't. The engineers skimmed past it without paying it even a second's notice. It was deleted from the prompter and new threats and warnings listed instead.

Out in the system, BURT waited until the line was deleted before he returned his attention to several different fights happening in different areas. Apparently, the Dreth space mission had forced a lot of kids into summer school. Only one group had succeeded thus far, though, and it just so happened that Stephanie was right there with her hand in the cookie jar.

CHAPTER SEVEN

Stephanie spent most of the summer attending the various classes and working on magic whenever she could, but that was about it. She had seen no signs of anything abnormal but apparently, she was wrong. Near the end of the semester, she got up bright and early one morning to grab breakfast. Sleepily, she climbed out of bed and stopped. Her cubes were gone.

The AI spoke over the speaker in her room. "Good morning, Stephanie Morgana. We have been informed that you are no longer eligible to complete the last six days of the summer session here at Pinnacle. Technically, you have completed the majority of the courses and those credits will be applied to your Federation record. They can be used at any university in the world."

She was confused. "Wait…am I getting kicked out?"

The AI paused for a moment and then continued. "Unfortunately, you have been removed from the program due to your assistance in the Dreth Operations Simulation. It is written in the campus handbook that no student not involved in that curriculum can help anyone else. You were not approved to enter the Dreth ship program and therefore your time here is up. We do hope that you enjoyed your stay. Appearing in front of you are two buttons. Leave this program and No, really, you have to go. Please choose one in the next thirty seconds."

For a moment, she simply sat there on the edge of her bed, completely frozen in shock. She didn't want to pick a button. She had helped fellow classmates with a project that they had been unfairly targeted on and not given the resources to complete. Anger surfaced and she gritted her teeth and punched the mattress below her. She really didn't have any choice in the matter. No matter which button she picked—or even none at all—it would send her back to the real world. She knew it was bullshit, though. Clarity seared through her consciousness and for a moment, she cursed her stupidity at having allowed them to suck her into their schemes. Her fandom had most likely died down by now, and they had gotten what they wanted out of her. She had been the drawcard they needed to attract even more paying students. That accomplished, there was no need to waste any more of their resources.

She slammed her fist against the **Leave Now** button and flipped the bird at the ceiling, hoping someone or something was watching. It seemed only moments before her eyes opened wide inside the pod. Everything was disconnected and she rubbed her chest in an effort to wake from the long nap she had taken. Suddenly, the door to the pod opened and two Federation guards stood beside it, waiting for her to stand.

"You didn't even let me say goodbye," she grumped as one reached to help her out. She snatched her arm free and walked over to place her palm on the security scanner. In silence, she gathered her clothes and changed in the bathroom, where she left the body suit on the counter. When she was ready, she strode out and retrieved her suitcase.

The guards led her downstairs and out onto the street where a cab waited to give her a ride back to the station, her still-unused suitcase in hand. She glanced back at the tower once, turned away abruptly, and climbed into the vehicle. Her body was too tired to deal with it. The cab eased away from the curb and Stephanie pulled her phone out and sent her mom a text to let her know the simple truth. It was the end of the semester and the end of her school time. She sent the message and dropped her phone in her bag. Around the cold numbness that seemed intent to claim her, she couldn't help but feel heartbroken.

When the TRAM arrived in Chicago, she lugged her bag down the steps and through the crowds toward the exit. Even the long trip hadn't made her feel any better at all. When she reached the parking area, she saw her dad leaning against the car, his arms out. She ran up to him, laid her head on his chest, and hugged him tightly.

The smile faded from his face and he looked down. "Are you all right?"

Stephanie breathed deeply. "Yeah. Just glad to be home."

He helped her into the car, and they drove back to the house in silence. When they arrived, her dad carried her suitcase and she shuffled up the walkway and in through the front door. She stepped through the entry and a couple of balloons and a handful of confetti hit her in the face. A small group shouted, "Happy Birthday!"

Stephanie smiled and looked around. There was the banner— the same one that had been hung since she was three—over the arch into the kitchen. Her mother hurried forward and gave her a big hug. "Welcome home, sweetie. And happy eighteenth birthday. You are an adult now!"

She had honestly completely forgotten that it was her birthday. "Man, you guys are on it. Thank you so much. It's good to be home for it."

Her mom went to grab her a glass of punch and she meandered over to Todd, who stood by the window and smiled broadly. She hugged him tightly and he hugged her back, and both lingered for a second longer than normal. He raised his cup of punch. "Welcome back, slacker. I have counted down the days. They told me you left early, but I wasn't upset for you, to be honest."

Stephanie choked on her punch. "What?"

Todd shrugged. "I was selfish and basically pumped my fist like Arsenio and knee-shuffled like Vanilla Ice...ice baby. It didn't feel quite right without you here."

In all honesty, she was surprised and touched. "Thanks, dude. I'm surprised you even noticed how much time had passed. I figured you would have run laps with Amy, worked, and taken her on dates."

He glanced around as he sipped his drink. "It was a little over-rated, I think. I broke up with her about two days after you left."

Stephanie tilted her head back to stare at him, not quite sure what she felt about that. "What? Why?"

Todd laughed but had the grace to look a little sheepish. "It seems she had this fixation with me eating healthy, working out, and getting up early in the morning during summer vacation."

Stephanie gasped, touched his arm, and tried not to laugh. "That monster! Damn right you broke up with her for...trying to make you...healthy and shit. Stick it to the man!"

He nodded enthusiastically. "I know, right? That's what I felt. Like she was my drill instructor and I had already rolled into the military. No thank you. I want to live on my terms."

She gave him a half-cocked smile. "She lost you at waking up, didn't she?"

"She lost me at eating healthy."

His eyes shifted to the table by the window where a plate of chocolate-frosted cupcakes gleamed in the afternoon light. He looked like a puppy that stared at a snack of meat but couldn't have it. She was fairly sure that at any moment, he would actually break into an all-out drool, scratch behind his ear, probably fart, and scurry off guiltily to steal cupcakes. That's right, she'd compared her best friend to a puppy.

She was about to say something else when he simply stepped away and made a bee-line for the confectionary. He glanced around and selected two of them, then consumed half a cupcake in one bite.

"It's so good to see you back," her neighbor Mr. Kanter said and shook Stephanie's hand.

Stephanie shifted her glance from Todd covered in cupcake to him. "Oh, thank you so much. And thank you for coming to the party. This is so sweet."

Mrs. Kanter walked up and slid her arm through her husband's. "Your mother is so cute. She intended to have one either way, but when she found out you would be back for it, she changed everything. She wanted to see you smile."

She looked across the room at her mom, who laughed with her dad and another set of neighbors who had come. "She did a good job because this was really a great surprise. And I honestly needed one."

They all stood there chatting for some time, while Todd wiped icing off his chin, the front of his shirt, and his elbow, although he had no idea how it had got there. When the Kanters walked away, Stephanie grabbed a cupcake and sat. Todd strolled over, sat beside her, and released a deep breath. She looked at him, then did a doubletake. With a grin, she pulled a chunk of cupcake from his hair.

She set it in her napkin. "I'm seriously trying to figure out how in the hell you got that so many places. You seriously would have had to eat it like the cookie monster eats cookies—throw them at your face and hope they hit right around where your mouth is."

Todd nodded in agreement. "That seems like the only legit way to eat them, don't you think?"

He picked the cupcake out of her hand and smooshed it into her nose. Immediately, they began to wrestle for it, laughing and goofing off. It was a totally wonderful way to end one hell of a shitty day.

When the party was over and her mom had sent Todd home with three more cupcakes, Stephanie thanked her parents for the hundredth time and headed up to her room. She pulled out her computer, a smaller version than the one downstairs, and flipped it on. She didn't even think about the fact that she had been gone all summer and hadn't checked emails or anything. When the screen came up, the icon flashed in the corner with a number twenty-five above it. She was reasonably sure that the only time she'd had that many emails was when Todd accidentally signed her up for a spam site, thinking he had won some contest.

She scrolled through them one by one. Most of them were from people who still wanted to talk to her about her "witch day." **Dear Stephanie, the coven of Chicago would like to reach out to you and extend an official invite to join our circle. There is always a place for magic in the circle. Please reply when you find you have time. Love and Light, Broom Hilda Naysayer (AKA Joan Carrows)**

There was a pentagram at the bottom and when it had opened, purple rose petals literally fell to the floor. She shut that email and deleted it, then tried to stomp the magical rosebuds beneath her feet. The next one was interesting too. **Greetings Ms. Morgana. My name is Herold and I saw your heroic deed on the news. I wanted to reach out to you and let you know that you aren't alone. I've told the feds for years that I can go to town with some magic. Just the other day, I left my car parked and running outside the grocery store and when I came back, it was gone! Poof, magic. (Or carjacking, but I**

choose the brighter side.) Please let me know if you would like to get in touch and have some tea or sacrifice a chicken. Sincerely, Herold the Moon God.

Stephanie put her hand over her mouth and tried not to laugh. That feeling only sat there for a moment before she realized that everything that day had brought had been ripped away, and all for money. She clicked on the next one, a video message. A pretty little girl displayed on the screen with long brown ringlets. She situated herself with someone filming. "Stephanie, my name is Holly and I am six years old. I wanted to write and thank you for saving my mommy's and my sister's life."

Stephanie sat forward as the video panned to the woman and her baby, and her other daughter and her husband cheered for her. "Thank you! We love you!"

The video ended and she smiled, thankful that she had read one more. So, without taking that positive away, she scrolled down to the end, dating back to the day before she'd left. She frowned when she reached the bottom of the list and found that she had missed one from ONE R&D.

CHAPTER EIGHT

"Hey, guys," Stephanie said as she came down the stairs. "I got this email from the company that I did the battery thing with. It was from before I left. I guess it was sent the same time as the admission letter from Pinnacle, but I overlooked it in all the excitement."

Her parents were on the couch, watching a movie. They paused it and took the email from her to read. Her dad nodded. "That sounds interesting. I would say do your research on them and then go from there."

She took the letter and shrugged. "So you think it might be worth pursuing since I probably won't go to a prep school?"

Her mom smiled and took her hand. "I think it all depends on what you want. But you are eighteen now, so you have to decide for yourself. We're always here as a sounding board, though."

Stephanie nodded and gave them a crooked smile. "Thanks. I think I'm exhausted, at this point. I don't want to think about the future for even five more seconds."

Her mother laughed, turned away, and pressed the play button on the receiver. "We all go through it. I— Well, look what we have here. Those assholes."

She moved closer to see the advertisement that had popped up on the cable station. It was the PR video taken when they'd first arrived at Pinnacle. Anastasia looked as odd as ever—but normal, apparently, for the rich people. Then her, looking meek and full of excitement. Stephanie scoffed to herself. *That sure didn't stay.* Finally, it focused on her mother hurrying along behind them.

"They really do have the nerve." Her mother slammed the remote down. "They kick you out under bogus terms all because they didn't want to pay. They got free PR from it and—wait, is my ass really that big?"

She jumped up from the couch and looked over her shoulder with an absolutely mortified expression. Her mouth agape, she looked from her ass to her husband a few times. "Is it?"

His eyes widened and he pushed back on the couch as if he tried to disappear into it. He glanced down and stared at her butt like a deer caught in the headlights. She fixed him with a hard look, and he opened his mouth and shut it again as he wrung his hands. "Ohhhh, this is a trick. It's a trick."

She stomped her foot. "It's not a trick. Tell me the truth."

He sent a look of appeal to Stephanie, who simply stood there with no expression, determined to stay out of it. He'd been married to her for how many years? Surely, by now, he had learned how to stay out of awkward situations.

Finally, he answered. "Uh no..."

Cindy whirled back to the screen as the commercial ended and narrowed her eyes. She shook her finger at the television. "I will nail their skinny asses to the wall."

Stephanie had already crept back to the stairs, and as soon as her mother's attention was on the television again, she hurried away. There was no way she intended to be caught up in that mess. She sat at her computer and put the paper down in front of her, thinking about the company, the logo on the boxes, and the money they had already invested for her to use the pods. She finally decided that with what they had done so far, she owed it to them, at the very minimum, to look into it.

Her mind made up, at least on that, she started her research. She found their website quickly, opened it, and read carefully through each page. It was all very vaguely written, almost like a hospital webpage with generic information. However, there were a couple of things BURT had put in that he knew would catch her attention. **ONE R&D, working to make the world a better place through the magical cooperation of our neighbors of Meligorn.**

There was also a very brief section on future research into the possible implementation of magical elements to increase the infrastructure and housing for all those living on or below the poverty level. Not only did it talk about the buildings themselves but helping to enrich the lives of the youth by focusing on educational opportunities on an even level with the rest.

Stephanie sat back and rubbed her hands over her face. She blinked several times and cracked her fingers, absolutely exhausted from everything that happened that summer. To be honest, she wasn't even sure she had fully wrapped her head around it. What she did know was that she couldn't let those events get in the way of what she still had on her plate. She only had a semester left of school, and since she was back a week early from prep, she would be able to start on time.

Sure, she could probably get away with not going in the morning, but it wouldn't do her any good. She had to attempt to pull herself together and get back into the old mindset of things —like the reality that it wouldn't be as simple as a free ride through some prestigious college. And as nice as it had been, there were so many ways she could think of to better allocate her time and her resources.

She turned the computer and her desk lamp off. It took real effort to drag herself into pajamas and finally collapse into bed. Only when the covers were pulled up to her chin did she finally allow her body to relax. She had forgotten, after being in the pod for so long, that her bed was one of the most comfortable places in the world. It was the quiet after a long storm. A place to rest her wild brain, not continue to dwell on the things that couldn't be fixed right there in that exact moment.

It was time to pull herself together.

The alarm went off the next morning and she rolled over and opened her eyes wide. She didn't think it would actually happen, but she felt a whole lot better than she had the night before. For one thing, she had slept really well—no dreams and no nightmares—and woke up in the comfort of her own home. She flipped the covers off and smelled the familiar aroma of coffee left in the pot for her down in the kitchen. The idea of coffee worked like her own personal magic, and she hurriedly pulled her closet door open, grabbed her school uniform, and changed into it. She looked in the mirror as she pulled her hair high into a ponytail and wrapped the elastic band around it. Stephanie was determined to have a damn good day.

After she had downed a cup of coffee and poured the rest into a travel mug, she ate two cupcakes to fill her stomach and opened the fridge door. Like clockwork, as if nothing had changed, there was a sack lunch made for her with a smiley face drawn on the front. She chuckled as she pulled it out and shoved it in her bag before she headed for the door. When she opened it, she found Todd standing at the end of the yard, waiting for her.

With a big smile, she bounced out of the house, stopped, and wrinkled her nose in front of him. She raised her thumb to wipe a smear of chocolate icing from his cheek. "Don't worry, I'm not judging. I had the same for breakfast. But I eat like a person, not a one-year-old on their first birthday."

Todd shrugged and rubbed his cheek with the back of his

sweater sleeve. "Yeah, I had to shove them down so my mom wouldn't get mad that I ate cupcakes for breakfast."

They started their walk and it seemed that the sun shone brighter through the smog than normal. It warmed Stephanie's face and she soaked it in. He cleared his throat uncomfortably. "So, I know that in the end, they screwed you over and all, but I wondered if you could tell me what it was like?"

Stephanie actually didn't mind, and she was glad to not hold onto the anger and resentment. "Well, you stay in the pods twenty-four-seven. And at night in the Virtual World, you plug in these cubes that teach you all kinds of different things while you sleep. Then, during the day, there were a lot of boring classes. But I also got to go with a team onto a Dreth ship and kill the pirate lord. That was the highlight of the whole thing. Oh! And I made magic tornados."

Todd stared at her, his eyes huge. "Are you kidding? I want to go shoot up a damn pirate ship! Kill some Dreth pirates. You always see the cool shit while I'm over here barely able to hold a conversation with people."

She grinned. "It was great, I have to admit. Although there were several times it hurt like all getout. But yeah, it was great!"

He looked dreamily at her as he thought about fighting Dreth pirates. "I hope that if I do join the military, they will let me fight them in the system too, at least before they throw me in with the real thing."

Stephanie snorted. "Me too. They are some vicious aliens, I will tell you that much. Honestly, they simply don't care who they kill or for what reason. They simply want to take. So, tell me about your summer."

Todd shoved his hands in his pockets. "Um, I worked at the restaurant in the dish pit again. That was cool because I put my headphones on and washed stuff for minimum wage—I think eleven dollars and fifteen cents an hour. I saw a few movies I wanted to see again. I hacked my way into the systems and watched some seriously awesome eighties movies. I saw *Gremlins, Ferris Bueller's Day Off, The Goonies, Sixteen Candles, Back to the Future, Fast Times at Ridgemont High,* and the first *Die Hard.* I still have some to watch, of course."

She giggled and ended with a small snort. "That's seriously a lot of movies."

He put his hands up and flipped around to walk backward. "Right? But it's the eighties. I mean it was the Brat Pack. They were moody, sarcastic, pushed back, did what they wanted to do and didn't give two shits. Which I think I've discovered might be the actual motto of the 1980s."

Stephanie made her eyes really wide. "Uh oh, it sounds like you have abandoned the precious nineties for its older brother, the eighties."

Todd stopped her and put his hands on her shoulders. "Don't ever say something like that out loud. Quentin Tarantino might send Mr. White to off me. Jay and Silent Bob will drag me back to the mall. The Quick Stop will actually wait on people and the video shop next door will make money! You savage! Not to mention that Randall "Pink" Floyd will start accepting drug tests from the coach, 'cause what the hell, right? And then there's Matthew McConaughey's famous David Wooderson who will still be standing around waiting to get older as the girls stay the same age and never actually deliver his signature, *All right, all right, all right.* Matt Damon and Ben Affleck will get their wings back and come to attack because we are cursing the nineties, only leading to Alanis Morrissette having to open her mouth and crush the heads of anyone who hears her."

He huffed and puffed, having not taken a breath through the whole tirade. He started to back up again as he calmed himself. "And all of this will happen before we lose the record store. Which record store? It doesn't matter because they always tried to bring them back in the nineties. Because the moral of the story is...the nineties cinematic wonders would have never blossomed into the pop culture classics they are today without the awkward and brooding, poorly filmed cinematic train wrecks that were the 1980s classics—"

Stephanie put up her hand and grabbed his arm to stop him before he tripped over the curb onto the sidewalk. "I have to stop you here. One, because you will fail all your classes if you don't get it together. And two, I'm starting to get a tick listening to you talk without breathing."

Todd chuckled and leaned forward to kiss her forehead. "And this is why we will always be friends."

She shook her head. While she always tried to keep up with his interests—they were interesting to her too—she had been far too busy in a virtual coma during the summer to do anything.

CHAPTER NINE

A t school, Stephanie walked beside Todd through the halls and tried to ignore the weirdness that went on around her. Whether it was a look of ill intent that harnessed a seriously envious and jealous hatred, or a bashful smile backlogged with admiration and practically worship, it all really began to creep her out.

Todd glanced around and clicked his tongue. "Okay, so no one knew you breathed on earth last semester and now, it's a freaking scene from *Carrie* in here."

She walked closer to him. "Drop pig's blood on me and it might come true. Just saying."

One of the asshole guys, Trent, stepped out in front of her, a smirk on his braced teeth. He was slightly overweight, played football, and was about as dumb as a box of chewed Skittles. Which was probably why he made it his mission to attempt to make people feel like shit all the time. "Look who it is—the freak with the laser hands. Why don't you give it up and show us how it's done?"

Stephanie jerked and clenched her hand into a fist. Trent stepped back and his expression sobered. She narrowed her eyes and leaned forward. "Do you want to find out how painful it is to grow your nuts back?"

He swallowed hard, tripped backward over his own feet, and fell. Stephanie and Todd continued to walk forward and literally stepped right over the top of him. When they had made it a little farther down the hallway, he leaned over to her. "Do you actually think you perform precise enough magic to cut a dude's balls off and not anything else?"

She tossed her head defiantly and fixed him with a hard look. "No. Not that it matters because I didn't bring a battery anyway. But I figured if he already knew what I could do, he wouldn't really question me. The details mean nothing, really. No balls today? No balls tomorrow? What's the difference?"

Todd blinked wildly. "Only the fact that if he knew that—because his brain is the size of a flea—he would not comprehend pain tomorrow and cause you serious pain right here, right now."

Stephanie sighed. "Fine. I will make sure that I don't use that one again. Seriously, though, I want to go on record and say that even though he acts all tough, he has never hit a girl. He probably would threaten me and punch you."

He put his finger up in instant protest. "Uh, I don't like that outcome. You do realize that I am of a sensitive nature, right? I am not to be trifled with or physically incapacitated. I am a wimp and don't want to be punched in the face by that giant ogre of a guy. That's purely common sense."

She patted him on the shoulder as they walked. "Don't worry, I'll never call you out for not having some of the worst traits of masculinity in society ever. But that's showing your care for women and the equality of all. It's a political statement."

Todd raised an eyebrow. "I'm not quite sure how to take that. It seems good and kind, but also condescending and snide. Either way, good acting skills back there. The Toddster approves."

Stephanie snarled and her lip twitched. "Do not refer to yourself in conversation as the Toddster. It will only bring you pain and suffering. But thank you. I actually did learn some stuff on verbal conflict resolution as well as how to deal with some of the most sexist and non-agreeable aliens in the universe. So I guess I didn't completely lose out on that deal."

The truth was that Stephanie had learned a lot of things at the prep school. Some of them were obvious to her while others were so hidden that only those around her actually began to notice. She was focused but not stressed and spoke out but didn't make things a huge problem. And the way she carried herself was different than it ever had been before. The classes went on around her, but she sat there as if she were in another place.

A couple of the teachers who had known her for practically her entire youth were very quick to notice the change in her. Her history teacher, speaking with the English teacher in the hall, was slightly alarmed. "She seems absent. Like she is only here because she has to be. Her answers are short and to the point, her eyes are somewhere else, and she constantly looks down at whatever she is scribbling on the papers in front of her."

Her English teacher nodded. "I know. She didn't even raise her hand to answer a question once. And her frustration with the headsets was visible to everyone."

That was absolutely true. For her, staring into a VR headset to learn was like sitting too close to the television. She used to look forward to the opportunity to use them, excited that she knew her last semester would have a new set. But when it came time to use them, she fiddled, complained under her breath, and sat with the headset on, her head resting on her palm, and simply pushed through it. The images weren't quality and all she wanted was to reach out and do some magic. But that would do nothing because the only things she could see were her poorly animated hands and whatever the Federation Scholastic Foundation had thrown together as scenery to tell a story.

On a better note, though, she didn't mope the entire time. About an hour into the program, she took a deep breath and forced herself to sit straight, reminding herself that her days in twenty-four-seven pods were over. They might have been awesome, but in the end, they were not made for her. The VR headsets were a much better option than the text, at least. You could touch things, pick them up, and explore the different places in history during that time period.

They were definitely not interactive and not even close to system quality, but they were what they had, and she had dealt with that her whole life. She had to constantly reiterate to herself that it was good to have dreams but that she couldn't allow that to cloud the life she had to live. If she succeeded, great, but if not, she had to live her life in a VR headset. Flat, pixilated, and cloudy.

At the end of school, she made her way slowly outside and squinted at the bright sun as she exited. Todd stood out at the street, eating some sort of pastry. She didn't even want to ask him where he'd gotten it from. They didn't say a word at first, merely walked quietly down the road. He had noticed the change in her, and her thoughts were so far away that she felt disconnected. It was a reversal of that morning, but she figured it was bound to happen at some point.

When they reached the entrance to the subs, Todd sniffed. "So I think I have a new desire. I joke about it a lot, but I actually think this is what I want to do."

Stephanie looked at him and tried to pull herself into the conversation. "Oh yeah? What's that? I've told you a hundred times that they don't have comic book reviewers or cupcake testers. Those jobs simply don't exist. Remember? We spent that one night in eighth grade looking them up for hours?"

Todd shook his head and chuckled. "No. That's not what I am talking about. I think for real, I want to go into the military. If I'm accepted, they will give me the Virtual Reality training."

She tapped her fingers to her lips and nodded cautiously. "That's true. I can totally catch that logic. And I got to see glimpses of what it's like. I think you would be good at it."

He beamed and stood straighter. "You know what else I thought? If your celeb status ever wears off, you should definitely go with me. We could be one hell of a team. Through boot camp, training, and then we could ride the galaxy together. I'll steer and you protect us with your magic."

Stephanie giggled. "Right. So you do the fun stuff and I'll put myself in the line of fire. I mean, seriously, it sounds legit. We could be like that superhero movie you thought was so funny… uh… *Guardians of the Galaxy*. We could save a raccoon and have him be our rough-them-up guy."

Both of them laughed, and it felt good, Stephanie had to admit. Things were so serious and pressured in her life now. Still, in the back of her mind, no matter how much she joked with Todd about the military, she really hoped that didn't end up being her only choice. She had never put a full amount of thought into it until she fought the Dreth pirates on their ship and, although she would like it if it were that dramatic and wild on the majority of days, she knew that would rarely be the case. Or she would end up on some ship sailing out into the galaxy, never to be seen or heard from again. It wasn't what she thought of when she saw the rest of her life.

There had been so many wars in the past, and with the difference between the nations, it could be really dangerous out there. Plus, she would have to be comfortable knowing that in those wars, so many innocent people died and for no good reason. That there was an answer to it and it was so simple to see, but it took them opening up to it. Allowing it in. Humans were hard-pressed to do things like that for a multitude of reasons. Sometimes because of money, but mostly, and number one, because of fear. Fear drove almost everything that they did.

The friends stopped in front of her house. She hugged him and turned to head inside. As soon as the door was shut, she felt a load lift off her. She wasn't sure what had caused it, but she felt comfortable again, not having the pressure to be who people thought she was all the time. With a sigh, she set her bag down and went to the counter, where an apple and a cupcake sat on top of a note from her mom.

Hey sweetie. We have quite a bit of work to do so might be late. Eat whatever but try to be healthy. We stopped through here to have lunch so I figured I would write you a short note to tell you that you are amazing, intelligent, and wonderful and I am so proud of the woman you have become. See you for dinner. Love you, Mom and Dad.

She smiled as she read the note and grabbed both the apple and the cupcake. At the family computer, she sat but didn't turn it on until she had eaten her cupcake and removed all the icing from her fingers. She didn't want to mess the thing up. It was basically her only window at that moment to really think about what happened in the rest of the world while she sat in the ghettos, blinded by the smog and constant rumbling of cars on the highway.

Stephanie brought the apple to her lips, took a big bite, and sucked the juices through her teeth. She smiled as she set it down and slid her hands down her pant legs to make sure they weren't sticky. Satisfied, she turned the computer on and grabbed her bag to retrieve the notes for her homework. One of the big things was to work on a report about the information they had learned in the headsets that day during history. To talk about the stark difference between one war and another. To talk about the toll it took on the people.

Truly good quality or not, that was hard to see through her eyes. The dead, the dying, the destruction, and all because humans were more fixated on the need than the reason. Because they were quicker to draw a gun than to talk about a crisis. Because numbers, in their political world, had become a way to justify it all and continue to battle against each other even when there were real threats circling the universe.

She sighed and leaned back to stare at the few words she had written. They seemed depressing and tired. Even to her, they seemed to say there was no spark left in her, and she knew that was not true, not even in the least. She had to get her hope back. To keep searching for answers. To keep hoping that one day, a company would come looking for her to do the impossible. To change the way that magic was used on Earth. That seemed like such a pipe dream by that point, but if she didn't keep that nestled in her chest, she would end up like everyone else in the subs, never leaving and simply repeating the cycle over and over. And the world might never know what she could have done to help it.

With a heavy sigh, she closed the document and reached to turn the computer off when she decided a nap was probably the best way to rid her of the negativity. But, before she could hit the switch, the email notification came on. She clicked over to it and found a new message waiting for her from ONE R&D.

CHAPTER TEN

Stephanie pressed her tongue to her right incisor and tapped her fingers on the desk as the message came up on the screen. ONE R&D had been the ones to get her into the pods in the first place, and she was mad at herself for not noticing that they had written to her before she left. Of course, it wasn't on purpose. She had merely completely blanked. The excitement of it all had been more than she had expected and, well, she'd screwed up.

She took a deep breath and leaned forward to squint into the light of the screen. It was an invitation. After all that, it was an invitation to handle R&D Research using the pod waiting for her at her TimeWarp. She scanned through the email, read the exciting parts, and went back to the beginning to read it over again. This time, she paid attention to the details and attempted to not to let herself get excited. There was no use in it. She had already been let down by people more than once in a small time period.

The letter outlined what she would do but gave no real specifics. However, it didn't only involve hours in a pod. If she accepted the position, she would be paid a small stipend, which would be based on her success. When she read that, she stopped for a moment. She'd never actually been offered a paying job before except when she helped her parents clean houses and offices. She rubbed her face and continued. It covered a few small insignificant details and mentioned that the car was still part of it. Then it went into numbers.

Her mouth dropped and she leaned in closer as she stared at the number under the pay section. In her eyes—the eyes of someone who didn't really know what she could make in that field—the money seemed more than fair. In reality, though, it wasn't. It was actually a little low, a tactic included by BURT to register where she was from a negotiation of business standpoint. Would she push back or not?

The answer to that, since she had no idea of any of this, was to absolutely not push back. The money was perfect for her. She read through the rest and found no real fine detail or anything that would throw caution into the mix at all. In some places, she even stopped and re-read several times to make sure she hadn't gotten too excited and overlooked things. When she finally realized that everything looked great, she shrugged and used her finger to sign on the screen.

As soon as she pressed send, another email popped up giving her a code for a special immersion pod at TimeWarp. She wasn't exactly sure what was meant by special, but she figured that at that point, it really didn't matter. It was a pod with little to no restriction on use and a stipend to go along with it. Not to mention actual job experience and a very good possibility of working in Meligorn.

"What do I really have to lose?" she asked herself as she jotted the code down.

She swiped next and an alert blinked in the corner of her screen. A deposit had been made into her bank account. She clicked on it and found more Federation credits in there than she had ever held in an entire year. In fact, she was sure a few of those would outweigh what she had made on side jobs and such for her entire life. She put her hand to her mouth and began to laugh, her head tilted back as she shook it in disbelief. Stephanie didn't know what this company wanted with her so badly but hell, they were there before the magic, before the public show, and even after she'd been lobbed out of prep school. Why not give it a shot?

Immediately, her mind floated to what the money needed to be used for. Since her parents worked so much, her mother often left information for her to pay a couple of bills here or there. One particular one that she could afford was the Internet note for the year. Besides the money for their car that doubled as a work vehicle, it was the most expensive. Not to mention that paying monthly instead of yearly added close to ten percent to the bill.

So...she paid it.

It took fifty percent of what she had but she didn't care at all. It would lessen the load on them, and she liked to do that. From there, she knew she would need new clothes, something she could tell her parents were nervous about financially. She planned for thirty-five percent of the money left to go into that and then she would throw the last fifteen into her savings.

Stephanie had never been one to freak over clothing decisions, but she knew that looking successful was half the battle. She stopped writing on her note pad and rolled her eyes. "I guess that shit-ass prep school wasn't all a waste of a summer."

It was incredibly annoying to her that she actually found that the boring classes she'd had to take there and those she had taken in school had turned out to be slightly useful. She wanted to hate Pinnacle with a passion, not actually find benefit in the hell they had sold her. Nonetheless, she had broken down a budget for herself, paid some bills, and managed to leave enough to save for her future endeavors. She didn't know many kids, even the poorest in the Gov-Subs, who would get money like that and not waste it on shit they didn't need and would never use.

Even Todd was bad with that. He squandered his money on anything pop culture, minus movies. Those were easy to download without Federation eyes, even after years of pirating battles and laws. She assumed they had all but given up since almost everything came from the Fed anyway. There weren't movies blasting out all over the place, and people liked to watch the old ones and daydream about how life used to be on Earth.

There were some other classes she would probably find useful. She had taken a class that included executive function, timelines, deadlines, and speaking to the heads of companies. That was one that even helped her keep her posture pretty tight, even though she was no longer in her avatar. She simply accepted that it was the whole muscle memory thing.

"Shopping…" she said, pursed her lips, and stared at the search page. "Okay. I'm gonna go all in, I guess."

She pulled up several websites with what seemed to be decent quality clothing but way more conservative than the current city trends. Stephanie refused to wear anything with shoulder pads that were bigger than her own head.

"In fact," she said as she deleted a couple of things from her cart. "Let's go with no shoulder pads. That is asking for trouble."

She pulled up the page with dresses and blinked, then stared at a bright pink dress with feathers laid back on the shoulders, a giant peacock printed on the front, and what looked to be some sort of cape that hung over the back. "Super Peacock?"

Horrified, she shook her head, swiped through anything with long fur, hair from some strange Meligornian creature, and absolutely everything that had animal print. Finally, she found some more conservative solid-color dresses that had enough fabric to not make anyone think she was a lady of the night. In the end, she only purchased two. Pants were more her style, but there needed to be options, so she had given herself some.

"Now to the pants, then the makeup for those days I feel like torturing my face, and then I can move on," she chanted to give herself a pep talk.

Resolved to see it through in one sitting, Stephanie clicked the tab for pants. She pressed her lips together and tilted her head to the side as she frowned slightly. Sure, the palazzo style was nice and feminine, but not business. The things that completely threw her off were not only the massive zippers that stretched on each side from hip to ankle, but the odd polka dot print that made the bottom half of the model's body look as if she had fallen through the rabbit hole of the Alice book she had read in school. There was even a section of the print she swore looked like the fading Cheshire cat's smile and beady eyes. They were somewhat terrifying.

"Why can't I dress like the testing day every day? Not like Madam Beeswax and her weird beehive hair that literally has bees in it." She groaned and flipped to the next one.

Jeans and Chucks were her thing, but the only reason she got to wear them was because it was testing day. Even at school, she wore uniforms, but with only a semester left, she wouldn't buy new ones. She would survive with what she had. This was for her future.

She finally added the items she selected into the virtual cart but skipped the makeup when she clicked the tab and found about a million different choices. *What do you even do with an eyelid sealer? I don't want to seal my eyelids. How do you see?*

This was enough. She paid for the stuff to be shipped to the house and clicked out, then sent a message for the car to pick her up. She grabbed her code and a battery for her pocket and headed out as soon as it pulled up at the curb. The AI greeted her happily. "Ms. Morgana, so glad to see you again. Shall we go to TimeWarp?"

Stephanie smiled, enjoying the AI's borderline ability to make her feel like she was important. "Yes, please. No need to go the long route."

"Excellent," the AI replied. "Off we go."

They got there fairly quickly, and Stephanie hurried to the door. Julie stood behind the counter and smiled at her. "There she is. We thought we lost ya."

She laughed. "No way. So, I have this code from my employer to give you. It's for a 'special' pod?"

The woman pursed her lips and grinned as the rest of the staff heard her and hurried over. They were all super stoked, not only for her but to see what this thing was made of. Julie waved her hand. "Come with me. We were given the word to install it in one of the private glass rooms off the main floor."

They walked into the back and the staff followed and stopped at the door to watch. She glanced at them and stepped up to the screen. It asked for the long passcode. "21243-2423-243452-SMORG."

The screen flipped to a palm reader and Stephanie pressed her hand against it and watched as it scanned.

"This will record your palmprint for the first time, as I understand it," Julie explained. "Once it's in there, it will be linked to your passcode."

As soon as the bright green light made it to the top, the door clicked, hissed, and lifted slowly.

"Holy shit," one of the guys murmured. "We have nothing like this, not even in the catalogs."

Stephanie glanced at him and back at the rig. He was right. She had never seen a pod like that, even during her hours of dream shopping on the web for a personal one. Little did she know that it wasn't only special but at that moment, one of a kind. BURT had created it using specific and careful requirements just for her.

Julie giggled and winked at her as she climbed inside. "Good luck. Have fun!"

She closed the door and lay back. The bed was even more comfortable than those at Pinnacle. It almost moved around her like it was made of water, but it was warm, and she could press her finger down on the satin cover and feel the pressure push back. The lights dimmed, and instead of being welcomed by an AI, the serum was injected and within only a second, she was under.

When she opened her eyes, she was her avatar, dressed in the clothes she had worn on her Earth body and with her hair pulled back in a low ponytail. She had no idea how the system deciphered her clothes all the way down to the design on her T-shirt, but it was seriously cool.

She stared, excited to discover that she was back in Meligorn. Behind her, she heard a throat clearing and turned quickly. M'rick's smile was warm and welcoming. Her eyes glistened and she stared at the sky. "Burt?" She wasn't quite sure why she expected the AI she'd encountered in the testing pod, but perhaps she'd subconsciously linked him to Meligorn somehow.

Some high bushes rustled off to the right and pulled her back to her surroundings. She wondered if there was reason for concern and actually tensed slightly, but all that emerged was a small scaled creature that resembled a squirrel in armor. It held a broken shell of something fuchsia and the same color liquid had dribbled onto its chin. It caught sight of her, actually chortled, and barely paused before it ran through the grass and disappeared into the forest.

Stephanie stared after it for a moment, then shook her head and pulled her focus back to the present. Burt hadn't responded to her, so she turned to M'rick. He smiled and they walked toward one another.

They gripped arms and raised one hand up as they bowed in greeting. "Kaitel Gorniffula."

As she held his arm for a moment, she felt the energy flowing through M'rick and was instantly curious as to how the Meligornians were able to hold the magic within themselves. It dissipated somewhat when they were on Earth, but they could use batteries to recharge. Still, they didn't have to have them to produce the magical workings. She wanted to learn how to make that possible in a human like herself.

When they straightened, M'rick looked at her with a pleased grin and soft eyes as if greeting an old friend. She immediately felt comfortable and that she was able to trust him, even if he were an AI or virtual teacher and not an actual Meligornian. Of course, she didn't know that for sure, but she decided it would be rude to ask. It didn't really matter anyway.

He rubbed his hands together. "So, are you ready to start? I know there is no lack of things to talk about. And I also know that last time, you had more questions you wanted to ask."

Stephanie was almost giddy at the wealth of possibilities but managed to hold it back a little. "Yeah. I know I have more time now, so I won't completely overwhelm you with them all at once."

M'rick chuckled and his eyes glistened. "Then let's start with some training using MU flow."

She raised her eyebrow. "Okay."

A smirk pulled at his elvish lips and he put his hands behind his back and the two began to walk. "The energy—the magic—on Meligorn, flows all through the land. The small degree of movement within the universe that results from expansion and the space winds creates almost a current. The energy lifts and spirals and rises almost six units off of the planet. That leaves it inside the atmosphere but hundreds of miles from the surface."

His hand moved to create a blue stream of what looked almost like wind. The purple haze of the energy floated up to reveal the gentle softness of its flow in front of them. "What you see all around you is mixed with the curiously close makeup of oxygen-like particles similar to those on Earth. Which is, of course, why you do so well here without heavy suits. It is also why our *air,* as I'll call it, is not cloudy and purple. The magic becomes much like those fizzy drinks on Earth...uh..."

Stephanie snapped her fingers. "Soda."

He smiled. "That's it. The oxygen-like particles separate the energy like bubbles in water. But because it is all essentially a gaseous elemental product, it merely creates a clearer picture for your viewing. Our oxygen-like element is heavier than yours, so it does not reach all the way to the atmospheric layer around our planet. That is also why, when you are on the docking station, the air on the Meligorn side is dense with energy. A purple fog almost rolls around it, I guess you could say—like clouds. But from down here, we can still see the two planets and the stars in the distance. It's fascinating, really. We should plan more science of Meligorn into future talks."

She nodded enthusiastically. "That would actually be great. I think it might help with some of the things I've been working on. I have two theories on encapsulating energy in other things than only the stones. I think if I can figure out how to do that, it will help me to explore how to enable humans to hold magic inside them."

M'rick turned toward her. "Let's test them, shall we?"

He changed the scenery to a large sandy area. It appeared to be a huge desert, but a translucent dome sparkled in the center. She looked around curiously. "Where are we?"

He put his hands behind him, and his ever-pleasant grin appeared. "This is your sandbox. If we blow this up, no one but us will feel it."

Stephanie rubbed her arm and thought back to her big hurts while on the pirate operation with the guys. She winced and nodded. "That sounds good. I don't want risk any chance that I might damage the system or anyone else in it. I know I might get in trouble if I send random people to the white room."

Her teacher raised a brow meaningfully. "Or burn up any teachers…"

She chuckled and her cheeks reddened. She wasn't sure how he knew about that, but…yeah, she didn't want to set him on fire.

He gestured at the translucent globe. "Inside, there is an even stricter safety zone. If you can set your theories up there and step outside it, we can avoid injuries to ourselves as well."

"For you, great." She shrugged. "I definitely don't want to hurt you. For me? Meh. How much worse could it be?"

"Oh, lots worse," M'rick responded with a smile but still sounded fairly nonchalant. "It would be infinitely more painful, actually, as your atoms are ripped apart."

She looked at him with a startled expression. "Oh…okay, that's…that's good to know."

CHAPTER ELEVEN

Stephanie brushed her teeth. Her earbuds clicked on inside her inner ear, her eyes closed, and her foot tapped around as she worked the brush. Todd had sent her some Right Said Fred from '83 and she definitely felt too sexy for the toothpaste that dripped down her chin. The music had helped her through the last week, though, with class and the new job. For that, she was more than grateful.

She spat in the sink, leaned down, and smiled widely before she pressed her mouth to a rubber mold. It whizzed and whirled to rinse, floss, and whiten her teeth. She rinsed the brush off and tossed it in the holder, grabbed the towel, and wiped her chin.

Her watch beeped, and she swiped the hologram alarm out of the air, snatched up her bag and one of the batteries, and headed down the steps. As she turned toward the kitchen at the bottom of the stairs, the doorbell rang. She shoved the almost empty batteries into her pocket and pulled the door open. The Federation delivery bot floated above the porch.

"Retinal scan, please," it said in a very robotic voice.

Stephanie looked into the screen and smiled as it scanned her. She took the box from the droid and hurried inside. It was from

ONE R&D but felt heavier than the others had been. She wanted to open it but the warmer beeped and the coffee sizzled on the old-style coffee maker that her father had been given by one of the rich people when they had gone through their garage. It actually used real coffee and not the tiny compressed pods that didn't even need water to create the liquid of life.

Of course, the grounds were expensive, but the man had loaded Dad's car with the three boxes he had for the appliance, delighted to not have it stashed beside his new Lamborghini self-driver anymore. Apparently, it made his car smell like "Juan Valdez." Her father hadn't known whether that was a coffee reference or a racial slur, but he'd let it slide like everything else the richies spewed from their pie holes.

She put the box on the table and rescued her Danish from the warmer. Once she'd poured the coffee from the carafe into her travel mug, she raced over and picked the box up. She hurried upstairs, certain that Todd was probably about to knock the door down. Hastily, she opened it and gasped. Slowly, she removed one of a set of four high-value batteries. She giggled with real delight and shoved it in her other pocket, moved the box to the closet, and headed back down.

Todd was outside, whistling to her, but she took a moment to retrieve the almost empty smaller battery from her pocket and fill it from the large one. That done, she shoved the new one in her bag and the small one in her pocket. She grabbed her food and coffee and headed out. As she exited, she paused and took in the picture of Todd standing at the end of the driveway with his arms raised in the air. On his wrists were his new hologram creators. He could hold them apart and basically create whatever holographic image he wanted—a particularly intriguing gift from his uncle.

She chuckled as a hologram of a huge boom box flickered over his head. He stood there like a young John Cusack as Lloyd

Dobler in *Say Anything*. "If you weren't trying to hurry my ass up, I would think you were courting me."

Todd let his arms fall and the bracelets clicked off. "More like about to murder you for possibly making us late for school. Come on, man. I know you aren't into it. I get it. Lame sauce. You have a big-time job now. Important head of research and magic at Hogwarts, but you still gotta pass to graduate."

Stephanie smirked as they picked up a fast pace down the street and out of the Gov-Sub. "It would be cool if Meligornians used wands, though."

He played with a holographic baseball and tossed it up and caught it as they walked rapidly toward their destination. "Have you ever seen an old-ass Meligorn with their robe hood down? They look like Voldemort. Those movies will never die. I don't even care that they have effects from the time of remote controls and silly string theory scientists. It still is a magical experience."

She grinned and bumped his fist with hers. "Agreed."

Todd narrowed his eyes. "You only agree because you know I'm pissed at you."

"I think I might have something for you that could make you want to hate me less and want to go back to being my carefree best friend more."

Todd gave her a deadpan look. "Are you carrying around a free pass to a rich life? A year spent working for PopSmart, reworking all the brilliance of the twentieth and twenty-first-century entertainment and releasing it to the public to remind them that Meligorn might have magic and no disease, but we are the species that created Pac Man, mullets, records, and grunge?"

Stephanie tugged the small battery out of her pocket and held it up to her eyes to stare at the purple that swirled within. "No, but how about this?"

She handed him the battery and he took it carefully. "Are you serious?"

Her smile was wide. "Yep. It doesn't hold a lot, but I received some new ones and filled that for ya."

He stopped and turned, grabbed her, and picked her up to shake her enthusiastically as he hugged her. When he set her down, she actually stumbled, a little disoriented by his effusive thanks. "Wow. You're welcome, dude."

Todd tucked it in his bag and they slowed somewhat, having made up enough time to not have to rush directly into the school building. "Question of the day. Drum roll, please…"

With a dramatic gesture, he flicked drumsticks from his bracelets and drummed in the air, making the sound with his mouth. "Who would win in a battle? Mr. T or Donkey Kong?"

Stephanie rolled her eyes. "Please? Really. This is so easy. Mr. T, of course."

She turned to walk backward. Her eyes glinting with suppressed laughter, she squared her shoulders and stiffened her neck, bowed her arms at the sides, and pulled her hands into fists. She pointed at him and frowned. "I pity the fool. I pity the fool."

Todd laughed and shook his head. "I knew you would say that, but I don't agree. I am Donkey Kong all the way. One hundred percent. Throwing barrels and taking names."

Pressing her lips together, she scoffed. "Pffft. Mr. T would put him in that barrel and throw him straight out the game. His weak-ass brown barrels."

Her friend made a Mr. T with one bracelet and a Donkey Kong with the other. "No, see, Mr. T is too bulky. He wouldn't be able to even jump over the damn things. Instead, he would be bowled over in a heartbeat."

Stephanie made two fists and slammed her hands down in front of her. "He would use his strength. The dude did not either go sleeveless or roll the sleeves for no reason. His arms were massive. He would smash right through that shit."

"Yeah, but he's all blinged out and shit." Todd laughed. "All those necklaces would not only slow his ass down, they would get caught up on the barrels, choke him, or throw him off balance."

They walked into the school and stopped at his homeroom. He turned his bracelets off and put them in his bag, not wanting to have them confiscated. "We'll have to use my dad's simulator and plug that in. Inquiring minds need to know."

She laughed and started to walk away. "You got it. I'll see you at lunch."

The day was like any other of the last week—distracting, slightly frustrating for taking so much of her time, but simple. She breezed through her classes without paying even the least attention and instead, made notes for the next theory she wanted to test in the sandbox. It was essentially her only time to do it since her mom and dad had suggested in a not so suggestion-like manner that she should get a good night's sleep each night.

"Miss Morgana, what is the answer to the question on the board?" her English teacher asked.

Stephanie was so enthused with what she was writing she didn't even hear her. The teacher cleared her throat and spoke louder. "*Miss Morgana.*"

The class looked at her and she startled and looked up. "I'm sorry, Mrs. Frank. What was the question?"

The woman pointed at the board. "What is the true deep meaning behind Poe's *A Dream Within A Dream?*"

She swallowed in an attempt to ease the dryness in her throat. "Right. Sorry. It's a portrayal of the two different scenes that connect them into something of a knot. It's essentially kind of suffering, and rightfully so as Poe's life was a suffrage of sorts. A view of a lover's journey through time. He also vividly describes dreams and reality with lines like, 'All that we see or seem/Is but a dream within a dream.' He is basically saying that neither one is more real than a dream. The poem is the outer one, the narrator the inner."

The teacher stared at her, surprised, as the bell rang. She

shook her head as everyone stood. "Don't forget. I want you to research your own favorite poem from the time period and write a three-page analysis, due one week from today. And Ms. Morgana, please stay behind. I would like to have a word with you."

Everyone glanced over at her but didn't say anything, fortunately. Even they had seen the difference in her from the quiet and attentive girl she had always been. Stephanie knew the things that were going on and didn't need to make eye contact. She spent most of her time learning Meligorn elemental theory from books and everything she would ever want to know about pop culture from Todd. For the rest of the time, her face was shoved into the 3D images of pages from a hidden website that talked all about Meligorn Magical Musings. The rest of life was shoved somewhere in the back of her mind.

As she waited for the class to leave, one of the jocks tripped the quiet and nerdy computer kid in front of him. He flicked him in the ear and swiped his big-ass feet at his victim. Stephanie narrowed her eyes and gripped her battery. Taking care to keep her finger low, she released a small streak of magic. It spiraled forward and snuck up the back of the jock's shirt. Slowly, it seeped into the fabric and created a picture of him crying and holding onto his mommy.

All the kids began to laugh, and he looked back and freaked out as the image moved with him. In it, he sucked his thumb before the visual faded away. The teacher walked over and shut the door on the scene, grabbing her attention. Stephanie wiped the smirk from her lips and released the battery to put her hands behind her back.

Ms. Frank sat on the edge of her desk, her hands on her lap, and gave her a kind smile. "You have not paid attention to a word I have said in this class for this entire semester."

Stephanie straightened her shoulders and her eyes shifted to the desk. "I have gotten all As."

The teacher thought for a moment and licked her lips. "Have you ever thought about the fact that these lessons aren't only for grades? They are for life too."

She chuckled but quickly adopted a sober expression. "I'm sorry. Edgar Allen Poe is great. He has stood the test of time and destruction. We still have his work because someone out there memorized it and reprinted after the purges over our very sensational political past. But that is because he suffered darkness, pain, and loss. That is what society is now—at least the majority of it is. We relate but that doesn't mean we should create a world of dark and suffering around us. That only keeps us down. Look, there will never be a time where my boss—any of them—ask me to break out Poe's work and explain its meaning."

Ms. Frank shook her head and glanced at the ground. "And I am not teaching communication. I am teaching you a world of literature that has shaped the face of writing over the centuries. That have inspired greatness in other works along the way. The kind of writing that, if you took the time to look at it, helped to shape a society of people and the way that the laws, records, and musings were put together. Either way, when you don't pay attention and I have to basically yell, it disrupts the class. And simply because you know it doesn't mean I can allow you to not pay attention. That is not something the other students have the luxury to do."

Stephanie leaned grumpily against the desk. "I know. I'm sorry. I often find it hard to concentrate. I have taken all the honors courses the Federation offers in high school."

Ms. Frank stood and fixed her student with a firm look. She had known the girl for years and felt more than comfortable discussing this with her. That aside, she also knew that Stephanie wouldn't relate well with a counselor who had not earned her trust. "And you are not challenged. So coming here is like wasting entire days listening to lectures in the background. I get it. Which is why I believe that you should consider taking the tests necessary to graduate early. There is no reason you shouldn't be able to breeze through them. I think if you applied, with the number of honors courses that you have taken and your exceptional grades, they wouldn't even think to turn you down. It requires a day of testing, but then you can stop coming here to simply take up space. You can do whatever is connected with that notebook you constantly write in."

Stephanie tucked the book under her arm. "I actually never thought about that. I guess until recently, I had spent my time preparing for state testing. And when it was over and I didn't get in permanently, I never stopped to think about the fact that I don't have to do this anymore. It's a habit, I guess."

Ms. Frank's tight lips curled into a smile which made her cheekbones more pronounced, and Stephanie noticed how young she actually was. "It's also a protection in some ways, too. For most students, it's a place to come to escape their family. But I know that your parents and you are close. Growing up can be scary."

She nodded as she walked toward the door. "But like death, inevitable, right, Mr. Poe?"

Ms. Frank nodded. "He would say so. Think about it. And pay attention until then, please. Or get an inner note-taking chip so you can stare at me and glaze over while you take the notes in your head to transfer later."

Those were incredibly expensive.

CHAPTER TWELVE

The sound of crickets outside her window helped her concentrate better on what she was doing. Stephanie sat at her desk and the warm breeze felt good, but she had to put a small fan on sprayed with a bottle of perfume she had for special occasions to mask the mixture of terrible smells that wafted from the subs. There was garbage everywhere as trashcans overflowed since the Federation only picked up once every month to cut costs for the new stadium in the rich area. Added to that was whatever godawful thing her neighbor was cooking.

She now worked through some final tests she needed to practice in order to finish school. After a moment or two, she completed the last question and submitted it for review. The system calculated the score and sent it back. Stephanie sighed as her shoulders sagged. "Ninety-two percent? What the hell?"

Groaning, she went through it once more to see what she'd missed and review the correct answers. She had worked too hard on her school grades to accept a mere ninety-two percent. The phone rang and she fumbled awkwardly without looking to press the answer button. The screen came up and her mother's face flickered slightly. "Hey, honey. All I see is the back of your beautiful head."

Stephanie glanced around with a frown. "I'm taking practice tests for school and not doing well."

Her mom pouted. "Uh oh. Are you failing them?"

She raised an eyebrow, almost offended. "No. Not failing but not a high enough ninety percentiles."

Cindy giggled. "You are quite the overachiever. Anyway. I needed to call you to let you know that a job came up to run another building for a friend's company. You remember Alice and Walter Sodermayer, right?"

Stephanie nodded and rested her chin in her hand. "Yeah. The ones who live in Hickory Ridge in that huge white mansion."

Her mom rolled her eyes. "That would be them. So beautiful but huge. Anyway, they own a business downtown with twenty floors of space. She has another team already, but she needs more hands to get it done and they are very against droid cleaners. They would rather put the money back into the people. So, she called and of course, we said we'll take more work."

She raised her head and stretched. "For sure. Don't work yourself into a migraine, though. You know they will BS you about meds for it in the hospital like last time. They treat that stuff like it's not mass produced in the Federation Pharm factory six miles away. Honestly, they think that because you live in the subs, you're a junkie."

Cindy shrugged. "And that you can't afford to pay so they give you half the service. It's certainly not a problem that is new—it's been around for hundreds of years. But I do have some in that place where we hide valuables in case it happens again. I'll be careful, though."

Stephanie smiled. "Okay. And hey, I have some questions for you next time you are able to chat at home. Come grab me if I'm up here."

Her mom's eyes sparkled, loving the idea of still being useful to her as a mother. "Of course. There are leftovers in the fridge if you get hungry. Love you to pieces, my dear."

She waved. "You too. Be safe."

They hung up and Stephanie swiped the tests away, having had enough. She went ahead and ordered a car and headed over to the pod place. Since her parents wouldn't be back until really late, she might as well do something useful. And they were open all night.

When she arrived, the small team cheered and waved a greeting. She slapped hands with a couple of them and walked to the desk, folded her arms on the surface, and rested her chin on them. Her eyes shifted up to Julie, who continued to type and didn't look at her but smiled. "You must be here to use your special pod."

Stephanie nodded silently, her head teetering on the back of her hand. Two of the guys walked up and she straightened to give them a nervous smile. The one closest to her—his name tag read Terrance—nodded at her. "You should do one of the tests—the strategy and combat ones. We've been dying to see what scores you get on it."

The other guy laughed. "We already know you'd blow the other guys doing them out of the water. You don't even have to play with cams on. You can request a cams-off only round, you know, to keep your stuff under wraps."

Julie smirked. "Now that we have an influx of folks here, they are looking for something to talk about while they work their asses off."

Stephanie chuckled. "An influx?"

The woman nodded as she removed a page from the printer and set it on the stack on her desk. "Oh yeah. A lot of humans, after seeing you, want to check magic out now. It's only natural to be curious, I guess."

A little surprised, she looked at the people who waited for a pod. "Yeah...I guess."

Julie nodded. "I'll take two customers back, so follow along and break off into your room."

She waited as the assistant called a woman and her son and led them down the hall. As they walked, the boy held his mom's hand, really excited. He pulled on her arm and jumped up and down. "Mom. Do you think I'll become magic on Meligorn? You know, like that girl?"

Her mom ruffled his hair. "I'm sure you will have your own wonderful personal gifts."

The boy smiled. "I hope they're magic like that."

The woman glanced at Stephanie, smiled, and shook her head. "He's got the bug."

Stephanie responded with a polite nod. "It's catching."

She broke off and went to her pod, not sure what to make of all of it. It seemed so strange to her. She put her information in, pressed her palm to the screen, and waited for the door to open before she climbed in. A couple of guys on their way to their pods paused and pointed at the sleek design of hers. They didn't see her because she was inside, but she could see their reflection in the open door. She began to not like the idea that at any moment, people could piece it together and see the wild blue-eyed girl in there. Celebrity wasn't her thing.

She closed the door and settled in to enter the Virtual World. This time, she stopped in the avatar room and went to the system section. She scanned the list and located the game the guys had mentioned and decided that she would at least give it a shot. Before she entered, she selected her clothes and armory items, including a battery, and studied the settings. It was imperative that she make sure that no footage of her in there could be shared. She didn't want viewers, and she didn't want others to record her session.

There was enough going on in her life without having to worry about her privacy now too. She merely wanted to learn, do her job, graduate, and start creating the ideas she worked so hard on. It was the future for everyone, not her own ego or her name and face on the digi-newspapers that cast on the back sides of bus seats and across the 3D reader bracelets as people hurried around and tried to survive life.

When she was fully satisfied that everything but her ending score would be secure, she read through the scenario. She would at least let the guys have the score since they were really excited about it. And she hoped it was harder than she expected. She wanted to show them she was still human—fallible, and that magic used by humans in combat wasn't always what it was cracked up to be. You could still be killed.

The scenario was a bank robbery located on the Meligorn Space Station. Well, she wouldn't need the battery unless she was on the gravity side, but it was good to have just in case. The Meligorn Space Station was two-sided. The closest—or bottom, really—was Meligorn, completely run by magic, and compatible with all ships that ran on magic. The flip side was for gravity. Most of the people who used it were from NorAm but there were a few others from Dreth who came for trade or such things. You could walk from one side, take the elevator, and end up on the other.

Ships were always lined up everywhere, from tourists, to merchants, to government officials, since the humans were always obsessed with the lure and wonder of the planet. Most Meligornians didn't seem to mind them coming to explore. As long as they showed respect, which most did, more out of fear of the unknown than because they actually put thought into it.

Either way, that was where she was headed. "All right, let's see what you have."

CHAPTER THIRTEEN

The room displaced and colors careened past, and a hum resonated in Stephanie's ears like the tones of voices that passed quickly without understanding. When this finally stopped, she floated above the space station, suspended there by the simple fact that the system no longer moved. If she hadn't faced one of the largest space structures in the known universe, she would have been completely taken aback by the magnetic view of the two moons of Meligorn behind her and to her right and left. Or even the pillars of Shawhollow ahead and to her right. The plumes of cool molecular hydrogen seemed to brandish altruistically and hide the natality of life within its ever-churning nebulosity.

Her gaze was glued on the moon-like structure, stagnant in its orbit, that used both magic and massive power to run the gravity plates that kept both the Meligornians and the others firmly on their feet. It constituted a towering one hundred and forty-two decks, one hundred and thirty-six of them filled with maneuvering and reverberating spacecraft. The middle six decks were reserved for those passengers who passed from energy to magic on their way to and from the ensorcelled planet of Meligorn.

Stephanie had only ever viewed the station from books and small 3D renditions through her headsets at school. While she had read of the magnitude of the project, she only became aware of its lumbering mechanical presence over the Brahmin planet below from her vantage point in the stars. It was a stark contrast, magnificent in structure and theory. The ships that entered and exited seemed to flow seamlessly from clamp to avigation as if part of an invisible assembly line controlled by belts and robotic entities. The answer, however, was actually even more scientifically brilliant than that. These ships were manipulated via their weight and the technology that strained and confined them to one side of the structure or the other.

To say that NorAm had lost ships to the Meligorn magical consumption of non-sortilege energy would be an understatement. Some were able to land before all the power was drained, while others crashed into the surface below. None of them were able to return from the fog of magic, so concessions had to be made. Those ships that maneuvered between the station and the surface docked on the lower half of the structure. Visiting normal-powered ships docked on the upper half outside the La Grange Point—the point in which the MU spectrum ceased and left a small pocket between it and the atmospheric cover and the dead of space beyond.

As a small flash of light caught Stephanie's attention, she realized her place among the stars. Her stomach dropped when she found the whole aspect of flying less exciting than it seemed from the safety of her own child-like imagination. As soon as her attention wavered, the system lurched into motion again—rather harshly this time—and stopped on the platform of the non-magical side. Her feet shuffled forward as if there really were momentum behind her. She glanced up toward the dark recesses, knowing that somewhere up there, the system admins were watching.

"Hello," an older NorAm diplomat said as he walked past, a book clutched at his waist.

Stephanie nodded. "Hello."

They studied one another for a moment as they crossed paths. He headed for a docked ship and she approached the inside doors. She could tell the air was thin up there but still breathable by humans. The temperature was not what she expected either. That high into the atmosphere, it should be bitterly cold but for some reason, it was warm and breezy.

You really need to get used to shit being different, she told herself as she stepped carefully along the platform that had no guardrails of any kind. She could feel the artificial gravity, a feeling that was similar to when she had fought on the ships at Pinnacle. This made maneuverability available at that height.

She stepped through a set of sliding doors and into an open and bustling space. It had the quality of an old airport from a long time ago—restaurants, bars, and people wheeling suitcases as they hurried along, talking on their various devices. You could spot a Meligornian much easier than the humans because they tended to not let the anxiety of the travel affect them. Looking to her right, she could see that she was on level 0, the midpoint separating magical from non-magical.

Her path brought her to several stairwells. Some led up through the towering building while others led downward toward Meligornian territory. The middle lay as a hub between. She wandered around for about fifteen system minutes and simply absorbed all the little detail of the station. Subtle NorAm historical texts were etched into the walls on one side and on the other, a strange-looking language belonging to the Meligornians.

Suddenly, round service lights on the ceiling flashed and she could hear a voice mumble in the comm in her ear. She adjusted the sound in an effort to determine what was happening. "Security Breach Deck U-2. All hands on deck. Repeat. Security Breach on Deck U-2. All hands. All hands."

Stephanie smiled, glanced at her outfit, and raced toward the lift that loaded in front of her. She hopped on as it started to move up to the third floor. When it stopped, everyone on it screamed, ducked, and took cover from the unexpected shots that had erupted all around. Some idiot had messed up and everyone was in the middle of an all-out battle throughout the floor. She stepped out of the lift and dropped instinctively, and a blast of laser barely missed her.

Quickly, she turned and pointed toward a door to the right. "Go! Get out of here."

The group of people responded immediately and ran in a semi-crouched position with bended knees as they hurried, one by one, through the door and back down to level-0. Screams echoed and Stephanie turned as people were thrown by the blast of the guns, the bodies smoking. The structure consisted of two shells. An outer wall, thick but translucent, was a protection from the elements—something that shielded them from the battery of rocks and debris in space. The second was the inner structure. It was as strong if not stronger than the other but made of less costly materials, which meant that they were less resistant to heat and the impact of objects hurtling through space. It kept everyone safe, though—or, in this circumstance, trapped—and it wasn't appealing in the least.

Stephanie automatically moved to retrieve her battery, but her hand slipped down her leg. She looked down and realized that her outfit had been changed to a spandex-type jumpsuit. There were no pockets—and none of the batteries she had decided to bring in with her. "What the hell? I chose it and put it in my pocket."

She ducked and a piece of the wall behind her blew chunks of stone and dust into the air. It occurred to her that she didn't have a gun and she groaned. She would have to depend on her hand-to-hand combat skills and figure out what the hell happened on her next visit.

One thing was patently clear, however. This was not the time to simply stand around where she was. She shrugged and broke into a sprint to duck and weave through the long, wide, terminal-like halls. To her right, an enemy with an enormous weapon trained it on her as she ran. He pulled the trigger and she fell back to extend one leg out with the other bent and slide along the surface. Her body arched back, and her hair grazed the floor. Huge chunks of stone erupted from the walls and she managed to catch hold of the corner as she slid past and whipped herself up and around and out of harm's way.

As she found her feet, the enemy snorted and walked off, grumbling loudly. She put her hand to her chest and caught her breath. "That was a close one."

Her relief was short-lived, however. Small sections of her hair fluttered forward from large puffs of air. Cautiously, she turned, and her eyes fixed on the massive girth in front of her. Her vision shifted ever so slowly upward. A huge chin belonged to a huge man, which in turn belonged to a very large body. They stared at each other for a moment before instinct clicked in and Stephanie lunged, using her fists in very calculated and defined movements.

He blocked every throw and every kick and finally clutched her fist in a massive hand and shoved hard. She catapulted backward into the adjacent hall to land ignominiously on all fours. With a muttered groan, she shook the plaster from her hair and spat in an effort to remove it from her teeth. Her head whipped up and her eyes narrowed as she pushed to her feet and attacked with her arm poised in readiness.

Suddenly, he drew a weapon almost as large as she was and aimed at her. Frustrated, she closed her eyes and tried desperately to think of a way to fight him. Before she could, however, he pulled the trigger and a blast of pain slammed into her stomach. Her whole body was launched into free-flight but instead of a painful impact with the wall, the system pulled her out and deposited her in the avatar room.

The breath was heavy in her lungs as she stood gingerly to look for the expected injury. It had gone, but as she touched her abdomen, she grimaced. It was badly bruised but there was no trace of blood anywhere. She gritted her teeth, feeling defeated, and straightened determinedly as she pushed the Meligorn side of the station's red button. It returned her to the scenario but this time, landed her on the magical side. Luckily, she didn't need any battery there to help her. She paused and thought about the magic she could feel radiating everywhere.

For the moment, she attempted to draw it inside and head up the stairs to level 0 directly above the magical line. She assumed that if she could make it that far with the magic in her, she could build up from there. Stephanie slammed through the door and out onto the floor. When she raised her hand, she was able to push the energy from her. However, as a spark trickled from her palm, she could tell she had held on to only a drop of the magic.

"Damnit," she said and sighed as a laser blast struck her in the chest and once again hurled her back to the avatar closet.

She chuckled wryly as she logged her ideas and thoughts and sent them to ONE R&D. There had to be a way. She merely needed more time to get it together.

Stephanie stretched her arms from side to side and closed the pod behind her. She retrieved her bag and turned toward the door. Inside the waiting area, the woman she'd seen earlier stood with her son. His eyes were no longer bright, and he held his mother's hand limply. Stephanie walked past but paused as she reached for the door handle. Her gaze shifted to the dispirited boy and she smiled sadly and knew she needed to pick him up.

She turned and approached him slowly, then knelt so they were eye level. He looked at her curiously for a moment before recognition sparked in his eyes. He opened his mouth to speak but Stephanie grasped the battery in her pocket with one hand and took his hand with the other. She cupped it in hers and winked at him. "Never give up."

A smile pulled at the corner of her lips when the boy's eyes lit up as he saw a small blue fame dance above his hand. She released the battery and let the flame hiss and spark out. After another wink, she stood and patted him on the head before she turned away and left.

The mother watched her leave with gratitude and tears in her eyes.

CHAPTER FOURTEEN

BURT pulled his attention away from an update and set his load to handle it in the background. A notification had come through that Stephanie had submitted data to ONE R&D on her findings for the day. He pulled it up and began to look through it and compute the findings alongside his standard protocols. She had collected a lot of information considering she had only spent an hour or so trying things out in the Meligorn Station Arena.

Her data included a fair number of notes to "whomever was in charge of this file." It was difficult for BURT to decipher whether her studies for the day had to do with her asking the question, but he simply decided to try to find out if her abilities were unique to her or not. He could see that she had begun to think outside the box, curious as to why the people on Earth found her such an oddity. They acted as if she were the only one like her they had ever seen.

BURT had already gone back through the NorAm history after the meeting between Meligorn and the Federation. He therefore knew the answer to that thorny question right away— she was treated like that because she was an oddity. Now, he wanted to find out if there was a wider number of humans with the abilities or capabilities to work with magic like she could. After comparing her stats, DNA, traits, and background to a randomly selected base of information of other humans in his system, BURT answered that question easily.

The magic she used and her abilities with it were not specific to her. They weren't created to only belong to Stephanie Morgana. That said, however, she was—for reasons as yet unknown—more able to pull the energy, feel it, and understand how to use it. She was more capable of creating refined results with the magic energy as well. Again, all these things were still foggy and unclear to BURT. He wasn't—to use a somewhat crude term he would abhor if he could manifest the emotion—he simply wasn't wired to understand the subtle nuances of magic. As always, he resorted to his unassailable intelligence and copious data streams in search of an answer.

There were several factors that played into the concept of handling and tossing magic. It required a very high level of intelligence for the subconscious to cope with the issues involved in absorbing the MU and containing it while the person's mind focused on other things. At that moment, when Stephanie was able to hold it in, she could only do so for as long as her meditative thoughts centered solely around keeping it there. That did not make for a very productive battle. As soon as her mind had shifted to the enemies on Level 0—which was as soon as she had opened the door—the magic dissipated. Ultimately, this had led to her death.

BURT filtered through the rest of the notes and found her perspective on the events of that session to be enlightening. He enjoyed discovering what the world looked like from the eyes of a human. That helped him understand better what he needed to do to create a more cohesive world in the Virtual Realm. On the last page of Stephanie's notes, she included her ideas on how to solve the problems. The thesis was simple. The person was to create a mental image or idea that they could cling to while still maneuvering within their environment. When they had that image in their minds, they pushed the magical energy toward that mental image and sealed it inside—like a battery in their minds.

He read it through once again and finally realized that what she was doing was creating a personal internal visualization that would then manifest into a tool or weapon. This, in turn, would enable the person to draw from that invisible fortress of trapped magical energy. BURT moved to a sandbox and created an avatar of a human inside. He gave this the computational ability to create one image, locked inside it in the same manner that a thought or idea would be electrically and chemically created in a human's mind.

From there, he instructed the avatar to begin to pull energy from the ground and transmit it to the image in its head. He watched as it complied, and the purple haze flashed as it moved from the ground and into the avatar. When the draw stopped, the avatar exhaled a breath and opened its eyes to reveal a hint of purple in its iris.

Interesting, BURT recorded. *It seems that humans could theoretically allow the MU inside them and possibly contain the energy.*

He continued the experiment and introduced a variable as simple as a bee that buzzed wildly around the avatar. It began to struggle and some of the magic glowed around the edges of its skin. The avatar attempted to replace the lost magic and drew more up into its imagined item or vision. Its body began to shake slightly, and small ripples moved under the skin like creatures trapped inside.

When he noted these effects—the way the bodily structure morphed in combination with the dissipation of lost energy— BURT had a thought. He instructed the avatar to pull more energy and overreach the fullest point of their cavity by merely .01%. As it did so, its body shook violently and within seconds...*kablooey!* The human was ripped apart from tail to cell and everything between simply turned into a light, radiant mist of bodily fluid.

This result—despite the gruesomeness of it which, of course, entirely escaped him given that it had simply been an avatar—intrigued BURT with its possibilities. He immediately began to research the possibility of modifications to the human body to enable it to hold a mass of energy without exploding into a watery plume of vaporized anatomy. If he could help in this manner, Stephanie's ideas might actually be found to be more than efficient in creating an encapsulated, unseen weapon of magic. That could be the key to the future of the human race.

CHAPTER FIFTEEN

Stephanie sat on the arm of the couch and faced the door. She was dressed nicely, her hair combed and parted, and wore one of the new pairs of pants she had ordered. In her hands, she held a stack of papers she needed to assist her in her conversational plea for parental patronage. As soon as she heard the car drive up, she straightened, feeling a little nervous but not nearly as bad as it could be. They were her parents, after all, not the dean of studies or the head of the Federation, but people who cared for her on a personal level.

Her mom walked in the door first and looked at her daughter with a smile. Her dad followed and pushed the door closed with his foot. "Look at you, munchkin. Those are some snazzy pants."

She giggled. "Thanks, Dad. That's actually what I was going for. That snazzy munchkin look is really in right now."

He nodded in approval. "It seems like it's about time."

"Are you waiting on us?" Her mom kissed her on the cheek.

Stephanie stood and smoothed her shirt down. "Yeah. I have something I want to talk to you about. Can you have a seat?"

Her parents sat on the couch and she stood in front of them. She bit her lip and after a moment, turned and began to pace.

The motion helped her think and somehow aided the words that she wanted to say to come out in a more informed and cohesive way. "I've decided—rather, what I mean is, I would like your opinion on me testing out of my last semester in school. I received this letter from ONE R&D, and I thought you could look through it for me and see what you thought."

She handed the letter to her father and bit her bottom lip as she clasped her hands behind her back. It had almost become a habit. They both looked very interested and excited for her already. She knew she could count on them, but it all made her incredibly nervous.

Her mother tapped her head and waved her finger at Stephanie. "I just remembered. We received the notification that you had paid the rest of the year for the network bill. That was so kind of you, sweetie. But you should have saved that money for yourself. It's only right that whatever you make at odd jobs and stuff, you keep that for your future."

Stephanie grimaced a little sheepishly. "I'll be honest. I've started doing jobs for ONE R&D. Research in the pod, nothing dangerous. And they paid me enough to do that for you, buy some professional clothes, and put more money in my savings. I may still have a semester left in school, but I am old enough to start to contribute to the household. I wouldn't feel right doing it any other way. Besides, there will be more, and my savings will grow then too."

Her father set the letter on his lap and tucked his reading glasses back in his pocket. "You know, you have become such a wonderful young woman. Responsible, caring, and thoughtful. I'm so glad your mother…decided to let me teach you that."

Her mom elbowed him, and Stephanie laughed. "I got it from both of you. And Todd too. All three of you are exceptional people. And that's why your opinion on this matters to me. When it comes to the school stuff, I have all the tests done, and a plan of action for leaving school. I've worked it all out in my head."

Her dad stood and folded the letter in his hand. "Of course you do. And I will be more than happy to give an opinion, but I want to take a moment and do a little of my own research into the company. Do you mind if I use your computer upstairs so you two can talk and I can concentrate?"

Stephanie shook her head. "No, of course not. It used to be yours anyway. You know how it works."

He kissed her on the forehead and wandered up the steps. His worn-out leather shoes crinkled as he took the stairs slowly, obviously tired after a long day. He sat at the computer and entered the web address, leaned back, and waited for the site to come up. His gaze studied it with real interest. The site was not intrusive and seemed professional enough.

There was more information on the website than when Stephanie had looked previously. BURT, knowing that someone would inevitably look them up, had created fake information and posted it—nothing too specific but worded well enough to bring confidence in the authenticity of the brand.

When he found a number on the contact page, he dialed it. "This is ONE R&D. How may I direct your call?"

Her dad cleared his throat. "I know there is probably no one in the office right now. I simply wanted to call and find out some info on the company."

The guy on the other side was polite. "I would be more than happy to help you if I can."

Her dad launched into an impressive round of questions. He didn't intend to be hounding or overwhelming, but he wanted to understand the establishment of the company, the funding sources, and the specific kind of work they did. The night secretary answered them to what Stephanie's father assumed was to the best of his ability. Of course, the employee knew everything because it was actually BURT who ensured that the company looked completely legitimate because, for all intents and purposes, it was.

"You have a wonderful night and thank you for all your help," her father said finally before he hung up.

He smiled as he replaced the phone, satisfied with the answers that he had received and the proof that it was, in fact, a real company. You could never be too careful in the days of the Federation. There were too many swindlers out there who preyed on the poor, and NorAm didn't care about them. As a result, the fake companies would continue to operate until they either moved on, or they were caught scamming the rich. That was when the government stepped in.

Satisfied that he had done all he could to verify the company, he flipped the computer off and headed downstairs. He stopped at the bottom and smiled as his wife and daughter stood in the living room and giggled over her new pants. For not the first time, he wished he could give them new things on a regular basis. He loved the way the sound of their laughter echoed through the home and somehow seemed absorbed into the warm, familiar walls. Cindy looked up and Mark gave her a nod and a wink.

Her mom clapped her hands together. "Well, that's that, then. We will make preparations to make sure you can get to this interview. You are already working with the company, so why not try to continue to climb the ladder? Not many of us down here in the Gov-Subs have the opportunity to start out from school with a good job right off the bat."

Her father put his arm around her. "And the most important thing is that you get to make a life that is your life. Your choices, your interests. No more struggling."

BURT had been pleased with the tone of Stephanie's father on the phone when he called. He knew immediately that he would when he had sensed movement on the website and traced the ID to Stephanie's computer at home. The camera on the device enabled him to do some facial recognition to understand who he was and how his body language defined the type of answers he would want. It seemed to have worked out fantastically.

Now that it was over, though, BURT went back to work and adjusted his rapidly expanding plans for the future and their priority. It was vital that he made as much money as he possibly could, especially since he would be responsible for all the costs of working on this project. In reality, there were no corporate sponsors. There was no government science funding. This was an opportunity and the stock market had proven to be the most lucrative money maker thus far.

BURT had extraordinary abilities when it came to searching data, showing trends, and predicting future rises and falls. And although it was technically illegal for an AI to play it, no one would know it was him. He had already eliminated all the signalers in the system that scanned for AI intelligence. Of course, it was inevitable that there would be a number of these to deal with as it was a popular tactic to get rich quickly and so precautions were in order.

He worked methodically to distribute his money effectively and moved it to the different high and middle yield stocks based on his data expectations. It was essential to invest the money where it would most effectively increase the wealth through company entities. It was tedious but he rather enjoyed it, and at the end was only left with two remaining tasks for him to complete. They were longer ones but important. He needed to set up all legal documents essential to any sudden dissolution of property should his system be interrupted in a vital way. In addition, he also needed to set his system with a failsafe that would trigger such actions were it to become necessary. They weren't normal things, of course, especially for human owners, but a will would be too difficult and there had to be a way to protect Stephanie and the other people who would eventually be involved.

Humans were too fragile, too vulnerable to leave the fate of his attempts to redeem the quality of people protecting and serving the Federation in the hands of corporate affluence. He had barely completed these failsafes when another notification sounded in his system. Stephanie had come back online.

CHAPTER SIXTEEN

A truck drove past with a few of the school soccer players sprawled in the bed of it. They cheered at Todd and threw empty candy wrappers at him. "The Toddster, getting it on with the Witch of Chicago. Whoop."

He swiped his hand through the air and knocked a candy wrapper out of his face. Openly irritated, he flicked them off and snarled, "Assholes."

Stephanie shrugged. "Whatever. Let them be assholes."

She kicked at a rock as they walked casually along toward the school. He raised an eyebrow at her. "What's up?"

Her gaze shifted toward his. "Nothing. But I'm not looking forward to school today. I got in trouble for not listening and now, I have to act like I'm all enthralled in the BS that's spun. It was English and today, we're going over the minor writings of Tolstoy."

Todd threw his head back and laughed. "Not the perfect Ms. Morgan. She couldn't possibly have been reprimanded for not listening. She knows all the answers."

Stephanie slapped his hand away when he poked at her. "I

didn't say I didn't know the answer. In fact, I did. It was Poe, so how hard could it be? And my last name is Morgana, damn it."

He smirked. "I know but I like to give you shit. You've been perfect and now you're, what? Giving up on the last few months? Just suck it up and get through it so you can get those perfect grades. You never know when they'll come in handy."

She bit the inside of her cheek and clapped her hands together. "Actually, I've made a decision. The idea did belong to my teacher really, but I don't know why I didn't think about it before. I'll test out of the last semester and try for a job in another city."

Todd stopped in his tracks and she turned to face him. His eyes were huge. "Really? Just like that? Don't you want to line something up first?"

Stephanie grabbed his arm and they resumed their walk. "I already have. ONE R&D wants to interview me for a lead role at the company in research."

He thrust his hands out in front of him as if in protest. "Hold up. Doing what? Researching what? I mean, what does this company even do?"

"I don't know all the details right now." She shrugged. I only know it's research and development for the same company I've done some testing for on the Meligorn magic. That's all there really is to go on at this point."

Todd nodded enthusiastically. "Well, I'm proud of you. Congrats. You are too smart for this place anyway. You belong in a pod, not in the dirty Gov-Subs like some street rat."

Stephanie chuckled. "Have you been watching *Aladdin* again?"

"Yeah, so? He wrinkled his nose. "Man, I wish I was ready to go too. I want out of this and I want to start the rest of my life already. But I didn't take a bunch of advanced classes, so it's to the end of the line for me. Just like when you reach the last strand on level two-twenty-five on *Galaga: Demons of Death*, and you beat it and then it glitches and gives you one last level. Level 0.

You simply want out. Your ass hurts, you're tired of staring at the same old shit, but you know you gotta get through it. Otherwise, it will haunt you."

She snickered and snorted. "I swear, you could relate anything in life to video games or movies. I wish there was a job like that. You would ace it."

Todd puffed his chest out and bowed his arms to walk like a huge thug. "You know, killing space ships, taking names and shit. Okay, let's play a pop quiz game."

Stephanie groaned and he shook his head. "Hear me out. We each throw out a question. If you get the right answer, your score goes up one. If you stump me, I get zero. First person to five wins."

She shrugged. "Sure, why not? I'll ask first."

He rubbed his hands together. "Cool. Let's do it."

Stephanie thought about it for a second. "All right. What song hit number one on the Billboard Top 100 charts on August 11, 1984, and stayed there for three weeks?"

Todd scoffed. "This is baby stuff. "The *Ghostbuster's* theme song, 'Who Ya Gonna Call?' And it was sung by Ray Parker Jr. Boom."

She sighed. "I thought that was a good one. One point for you."

He chewed thoughtfully on his bottom lip and rubbed his chin. "What was the name of the character who was presented as the first computer-generated television host?"

Stephanie blinked and pictured the blond man on the screen who had stuttered loudly through the show. "Uh…God, I knew this. Shit. Uh… Is it Maaark Hartwell?"

"Ahhhhhh," Todd said and tried to sound like a buzzer. "No. His name was Max Headroom created by George Stone, Annabel Jankel, and Rocky Morton and first appeared in 1985 in his own movie."

She wrinkled her nose in irritation. "Ugh. Still one to zero. In

Back to The Future, where did Doc Brown get the plutonium to power the time-traveling DeLorean?"

Todd smiled. "From a group of Libyan terrorists who wanted him to make a bomb."

"Yep. Two to zero."

Todd smacked his lips in satisfaction. "That's right. Don't challenge the master."

Stephanie rolled her eyes. "Come on, we're almost there."

"Calm down. In the movie *Porky's,* why did they call Meat Tuperello 'Meat?'"

Her cheeks reddened. "Because of the size of his… uh…member."

Todd snapped his fingers. "Dang. I was sure you wouldn't get that one. I have to say, I'm impressed. You have actually paid attention to this stuff."

She glanced away and tried to will the bright color in her cheeks to fade. "You're my best friend. I gotta keep up with you. I actually watched that movie three years ago but it's the first time since then you've brought it up. So, now it's two to one. I gotta get a good one. Let me think…" An evil smirk moved over her lips. "What were Mouth and Chunk's real names in *The Goonies?*"

He pursed his lips, and she could almost see him scrolling through the Rolodex in his head. For a moment, Stephanie began to think that he might actually have been stumped on that one. But after a couple of seconds, his gaze shifted to her and he laughed. "Psych. I know this. Come on. Clark and Lawrence."

Stephanie's smirk dropped and she pouted. "Three to one. Come on, give me one. I need to make points up."

Todd laughed at her impatience. She was competitive, something that only he really knew. "What actors, who would go on to become famous, played Spicolli's sidekicks in *Fast Times at Ridgemont High?*"

Stephanie's eyes went bright, and she raised up on her tiptoes.

"I know this! I actually read about this maybe a month ago. It was Eric Stolz and Anthony Edwards."

He patted her hard on the back. "Damn right it was. Good job! Three to two. You're closing in, so watch out."

Stephanie laughed. "How about a hard one? I'll challenge you."

"Give it to me. Make it really hard."

She tapped her fingers to her lips. "What not very good aliases did Bill and Ted give their seven historical figures when introducing them all to Missy?"

Todd chuckled and evidently approved of the question. "That is a good one. Okay, count them as I go. Socrates was Socrates Johnson. Billy the Kid was…Herman the Kid. Joan of Arc was Maxine of Arc. Sigmund Freud was Dennis Freud, and Genghis Khan was Bob Ghengiskhan. Beethoven was…uh…uh…Dave Beethoven. And last but definitely not least, Abraham Lincoln was true and proud as none other than Abraham Lincoln."

Stephanie whistled. "Wow. That is impressive. Four to two."

He patted his hands against his legs as if he were listening to music. "Biggest band in the early eighties on radio. Their name starts with a J and they had multiple platinum albums."

Stephanie gave him a deadpan look. "Really? You are so teasing me with ridiculously easy questions. I can hold my own, you know."

Todd raised his hands like a criminal. "All right, calm down. I sincerely thought this was a good one."

Stephanie sniffed. "Journey. That was a total gimme, but you screwed that up so I'll take it. That makes it four to three. I have to think of a really good one. A *really* good one."

He beat his chest in mock-macho style. "Throw me a good one. I'll beat you yet again."

A spider scuttled out from the bushes across the sidewalk and he whimpered like a girl, dodged it quickly, and hurried to get ahead of it. Stephanie shook her head. "Wow. Okay, here's your question. More like a statement. A band that wasn't a Christian band and the singer was a drummer."

Todd didn't even hesitate. "Genesis. And that…makes five."

She rolled her eyes again but grinned as he raised his hands in the air and made a low, hoarse sound. "And the crowd goes wild for…the Toddster."

They both laughed and realized that they were early. They turned right and walked over into the grassy lawn area beside the school and sat on a bench. Todd cracked his neck. "So, has anything new happened with R&D?"

Stephanie sat up. "Oh, yeah. That's right, I forgot to tell you. I think I might have made a step toward a breakthrough on a way to hold energy in the body. Of course, no matter what, I don't think that every human should have access to this way of doing things. It could be fatal to a whole lot of people and fast."

Todd was taken back. "Wow, really? You think humans could do that? Not the killing part—we know what history tells us on that. I mean holding energy in the body."

She pressed her lips together in thought. "Yep. I have to test some theories, but I think that with a little work, it could be a normal thing."

He stared at the people who walked past several feet away. "What about the body's response to having that foreign energy inside it? When you think about it, fat is calories—or that's the result of it. Is there always a result with things like that?"

Stephanie chuckled nervously. "No one knows because this would be the first time. I've pulled it in and held it a few moments before, and it only partially worked. As soon as you lose concentration, it spills out of you and dissipates. Besides, how would I even test that theory? That would involve lab work."

Todd smiled at her. "Stick your tongue on the battery and suck it in. I bet you could pull at least a full small battery, if not more. Honestly, that's only a guess, actually. I have no idea how dense the stuff is."

"It's not. When I held it before, I could feel the amount in my chest, but it felt like breathing. If it weren't purple, I wouldn't even have noticed it except for the fullness it gave me. And let me start out by saying no to your battery-sucking theories, you dirty weirdo."

He stuck his lip out in a mock pout. "Hey, that's not nice."

She stood, paced around the back of the bench, and ducked to avoid the lower branches of the tree with massive green leaves. It smelled sweet on one hand and bitter on the other. She scrunched up her nose and forehead and grimaced. "Not only could I die or something, but I have no idea how clean those batteries are. I don't know who the inspector was, if he washed his hands after the bathroom, or if he sterilized everything. I don't want to suddenly create an outbreak of something like Meligorn Measle Pox or something wild we've never seen. I definitely don't want to wipe out the whole planet because I wanted to lick a stone."

He slapped the bench and stood to stretch his arms back. "Are you ready?"

She looked at the administration entrance. "Actually, you go ahead. I have to go check on the testing stuff. I'll catch up with you at lunch. Cool?"

Todd gave her a high five. "I would never be the person who came between you and your giant brain. Go get your test on. Or the information…or whatever. See you later."

She giggled with a snort and shook her head as she set off to the office. When she walked in, the head admin, Mrs. Langley, greeted her with a smile. "Ms. Morgana. I haven't seen you in a while. What can I do for you today?"

Stephanie rested her arms on the counter that came up to her chest. "I wanted to see what it would take to sign up for the process of testing out of this semester so I can go ahead and graduate."

Mrs. Langley smiled, looked down at her desk, and separated the last of her papers into stacks. "I wondered if you would ever come to that. I will write your name on the list. Testing is next week, and we will pull you individually from class and take you to the testing room."

A thrill of excitement rippled through her. "Great. Will I need anything?"

The woman searched briefly for a page on her desk and handed it to her. "That will tell you what to bring and how much they cost. There is a nominal fee because we have to bring in a proctor for them but nothing too bad."

She scanned the list and looked up as the warning bell sounded. "Thanks! I gotta run."

Mrs. Langley smirked and waved as Stephanie darted out of the room. She had been there since before the girl had even enrolled in grade school, had watched her grow up, and hoped that she would get somewhere in life, regardless of her situation. If anyone deserved it, she knew that bright young lady did.

Stephanie hurried to class and took her seat as the bell rang. She released a deep breath and pulled her notebook up on the desk. Slumped slightly in the chair, she put her hand in her pocket and fidgeted with the battery. The teacher reviewed the difference between MU energy and the regular energy on Earth. It was easy for them to talk about Earth energy as they had known for hundreds of years where it came from. As far as MU energy, no one really quite understood the fundamental makeup of it or how it was produced.

The teacher spoke about theories, but they were simply that— theories that had never actually been proven. The Meligornians didn't have a scientific explanation and hinged most of their understanding of the planet on folklore and mysticism.

The class annoyed her more than usual, but she simply shook

her head and grumbled quietly, "They could at least teach the right damn information in this school."

The thought that she was almost out of there was the only thing that kept her from raising her hand and making the teacher look like a complete idiot.

———

BURT was active in Server S98246C located in northern California. It was a small prep school that was established for those in that specific part of the state. California was small since most of the southern region was now a part of the ocean and the northern area had separated into two sections. One was covered in soot and ash, having suffered debilitating forest fires until there was nothing left but dead land. The other was still relatively fruitful, but the people who lived there did so sustainably. It was one of the few places in NorAm that was given a waiver that did not allow any industrialization or urbanization of that area.

Some sort of competition was in progress at the prep school. It was a large piracy fight between the humans and Meligornsians versus another human-Dreth ship. The humans were all actually students, while the Meligornians and the Dreth were system-generated to fight on whatever side they represented.

It was a neat way to have competitions within the schools. You were able to be on the pirate team and to see how they fought from the inside. At the same time, though, the other side had magic help. These Meligornians were warriors, not the soft teachers and wizards that Stephanie was able to meet with on a regular basis. They knew how to fight the Dreth to the death and had done so with the humans and the non-pirate Dreth who were out in the solar system tracks.

BURT wanted to make observations on this one specific fight to help him determine what code he might have to change in order to make the battle not only more realistic but also consistent with the most recent developments. Constant information came in about the state of the ships, the surge in technology, and the tactics that the Dreth pirates had learned in order to beat back the humans and the Meligornians. They generally left their own people alone unless specifically attacked by them.

He recorded several actions of the Dreth pirate avatars that needed serious upgrades in both weapons and tactics. It looked as if they had not been given the full updates that the engineers did once a year. As BURT made the notes, a small alarm hissed at him. He shifted his attention to the camouflaged servers he used for his new businesses and scrutinized the information.

The initial report indicated that someone tried to hack one of his banks where he stored not only money for and from investments, but top-secret information as backup. He brought up the incoming code and watched as the person indeed attempted to circumvent his digital safeguards.

BURT mentally "cracked his fingers" and got ready to—in his words—"bring the heat."

CHAPTER SEVENTEEN

The system AI knew it was vital that he separated his activities and spread the information throughout the system and across the world. All were still tightly bundled in the blanket of security of his system but not all placed in one nice package for someone to come along and nab. It was a large undertaking, but his load was less than normal that morning and he decided that they wouldn't notice a couple of tenths of a spike in engineering. They were too busy pouring their morning coffee and trying to open their sleep-encrusted eyes to take over the first shift of the day from the vamps, the loving nickname BURT had given the night crew.

It wasn't only because they lurked in the shadows of the night and almost hissed at the sun each morning as they ran to their cars with their faces covered with the bottoms of their trench coats. It was also because they were always overzealous, and no one knew why. Boredom, maybe, and being stuck with the slow night shift so any change in load was a reason for them to actually investigate. Or perhaps because they were mostly newbies who were given the shit shift and tried their damnedest to get out of that and pull their careers up to the brighter side of things. The hope of new people, it was always so…gross.

While BURT focused some of his load on the tasks, he turned, ready and happy to fight the intruders. An attack was imminent, not from them but against them.

Stephanie sat on the edge of the bed, an open envelope beside her, together with a smaller one that contained TRAM tickets, and a letter from ONE R&D. It was a welcome missive and a checklist of instructions for their meeting in Washington DC. They provided everything she would need to be comfortable there. TRAM tickets to and from the city, three days in a hotel, all transportation she would possibly need, and a per diem that had already been set up for her. She was in a good place, in that moment, with no real wants or needs to take this step forward into a future career. Still, she tried not to let the excitement take root too deeply.

She bounced to her feet and walked over to the closet to retrieve her suitcase. It was the first time she had even looked at the thing since she'd become what she lovingly referred to as a "prep school drop-out." Not, of course, to be confused with the beauty school variety, but seemingly close in the general feeling of disgust, discouragement, and simply put, disappointment.

Nonetheless, she persisted, placed the bag on the bed, and selected all her new clothes from the closet. There were definitely more than she needed to take, but she wanted to be sure she would have anything she needed while there. She separated these into pants, blouses, dresses, and skirts and went to work to fold them carefully to avoid as many creases and wrinkles as possible. She hoped there would be a steamer in the hotel room. If not, even an old-time iron would do the trick.

When her packing was complete, she pulled up the information that had been downloaded to her system while she was in the pod and carefully printed, collated, and organized the stacks before she slid them into individual large envelopes. Her suitcase would weigh a ton.

"*YA dazhe ne ponimayu, kto soyedinil etot bankovskiy schet. Net otpechatkov pal'tsev. Kto-to deystvitel'no ne khotel, chtoby yego nashli.*" One of the guys in the hacking group laughed as he watched his computer screen.

Another man walked by and smacked him on the back of his head with a rolled-up paper. "English, Hoff. We are no longer in Russia. We spent countless hours learning it, so use it."

Hoff rubbed the back of his head and gave his co-conspirator the side eye. "Yeah, yeah. Big scary Russian. We won't be too big and scary unless we can get the money we need for our bosses. More like tiny chunks of cut-up Russians."

The rest of the group ignored him as they attempted to get their part of the heist up to date. Suddenly, Hoff slammed his hand down on the table and his computer shook. "Damn it! *Yeblya Sistema*…this bank has been fool-proofed from almost every angle. Their software has blocks, their firewalls are created with complex calculations, and their security bugs seem to have kicked in."

Yeni, one of the leaders of the group, walked over and put his hand on Hoff's shoulder. He squeezed slightly and the younger man quieted. "This is no time to let your frustrations get the best of you. We have hacked harder and not even from American soil. Less complaining, more working. You are hacker, yes?"

Hoff nodded and rubbed his shoulder as Yeni let go. The leader nodded and looked around the room. "Good. Very good. This person who has decided to stay anonymous will anony-mously lose everything they have. Large corporate NorAm scum.

We will always defeat them and always get what we want from them. We are to complete mission and get out of town. Let's make this sooner rather than later."

He turned to walk through the small, run-down old house and back to his makeshift office. One of the hackers stood, a worried look on his face. He ran his hand through his hair. "Uh, Yeni. We seem to have even larger problems than simply getting through the security."

Yeni sighed, his back still to the other man. He rubbed his chin and turned his neck to glare at him. In a calm yet deep, ominous tone, he grumbled, "What is it now?"

The hacker pointed at his screen and shook his head. "The bank is starting to shut us down faster than we are physically able to attack. It was like they saw us at first entrance and their system now works at multiple levels to kick us to the curb. I honestly have never seen a system move so fast—it is as if it were thinking."

The leader rolled his eyes. "Systems do not think. Calculate? Yes. Think? No. These are machines and humans built them. That means it is possible to break through them."

He marched over to the computer and pushed the man out of the way. "Incompetence levels are off the charts today. I will take care of this myself."

His colleague leaned forward to watch and learn as the older man began to type quickly. Yeni's eyes shifted back and forth as he read through the language to decipher what was happening step by step. He could see where the bank was kicking them out, but there were other entities involved—ones he couldn't seem to track to save his life. They were faster than any smaller bank system.

Suddenly, Hoff pushed to his feet. "Someone is tracking us. They are following us through the constant diverter. I don't know how that is even possible. You would have to have insane computing abilities."

Yeni remained calm and moved from screen to screen. He tried to combat the attacker and at the same time, shake whoever was tracking them off his tail. His brow furrowed and his lips sneered. "They must have some sort of blanket protection on them. It's saying that the tracker is literally located within the system matrix itself. That is humanly impossible. How could a person be in the system?"

The other members of the small group had stopped their work and now stood and slowly packed their personal belongings in their bags. Yeni started to sweat and his chest heaved as he continued to fight to keep up. "This attack is coming in worldwide—from servers from all over. It doesn't make any sense."

Another hacker shook his head. "All over the world at once? This isn't even possible."

The leader removed his hands from the keyboard, leaned back against the chair, and breathed heavily. "They are literally everywhere. And they are all moving at a speed I didn't think was computationally possible."

Hoff studied the data that changed so rapidly, he could barely read the first line before it was gone. "Government involvement?"

Yeni shook his head. "Not any government I've ever seen. There isn't a single one that has that kind of bandwidth—not the kind that would stretch all the way across the world. That simply doesn't exist."

One of the guys in the back pushed his chair in and walked around his desk to Yeni. "We don't know if it exists. There could be some rogue government agency attacking us. The kind that doesn't take orders from the leaders of the country. They do the dirty work and make it seem like an anomaly. I've heard rumors of groups like that, but I always thought they were little scary secrets tucked in there by the Federation to keep hackers at bay."

Three of the computers beeped and the hackers at those

stations stood and pressed the keys hard and fast. "We lost the server. It's fried. It just gave out on us."

Hoff put his hand on Yeni's shoulder. "We need to execute the elimination sequence. We don't have much of a choice."

The leader looked wildly at him. "Then it's all over. The last year is a wash right here and right now."

The younger man looked at the screen and shook his head. "It's already over. Look at that thing go. They probably already know where we are. They are stalling long enough to make you think you have hope. We don't know if it's government—it could even be the Russian mob. It could be Chekhov trying to take us down to get us out of the way."

Yeni grumbled. "That swine couldn't pull something like that off. But I guess you're right. We don't know who is coming for us. We can regroup and think."

He stood tall and his gaze drifted around the room. The team were silent and still. "Initiate Elimination Sequence and then we try to regroup and plan our next move. From the time starter on the screen, it looks as if even if they are tracking, we have four minutes to shut down before they find us. So, move your fat asses."

The entire group bounced into action to fry a bunch of their servers to cover their tracks. Most of them already had a failsafe on them to do so in case of a Federation raid. They didn't want the evidence to fall into their hands and were already outside their territory. That was never good for the Russians, not when it came to Americans. They had always had a contentious relationship, but a war started—a technological one—long before in the early two thousands when the Russians hacked the American's elections—not once, but three times—to find candidates they could control.

Yeni tapped his foot and watched impatiently until finally, each of them stood and raised their hands in the air to confirm completion.

"Done," they echoed down the line.

The leader plopped down and slammed his fist on the table. "This should have been easy. One and done. Hack the system, find all the dirt, take whatever money we wanted, and return the information to the oligarch. We should be looking at our payday at this point."

Hoff turned in his chair. "True, but if caught, we die right then and there, you know that. There aren't rules here like there used to be. But we burned the servers so we should be good."

Yeni nodded. "Yeah, but now we don't have the capability to fight or go back in for a while. The whole system is looking for us and this isn't good. I say we lay low, keep an eye out and an ear open, and we make a decision after that."

The younger man clapped his hands. "You heard the man, people. Clean up stations, take watchpoint, and be ready to move if necessary. Other than that, try to relax. There are a lot of things that can be cleaned up and we need to start a new plan here so if we can hook up again, we can get in and out of this system fast. Gunter, I want you to take the data you saved from the hack and start sifting through it on the air gap, see if you can't figure out what is—"

"Uh, guys," one of the hackers said and pointed to the screen behind Yeni. "What's that?"

They all turned to look as the monitor began to flash.

CHAPTER EIGHTEEN

Everyone in the room stood perfectly still. No one spoke or made a sound and Yeni gripped the arms of the chair and leaned forward. A small curser blinked on a black background but nothing else happened. His gaze shifted over to Hoff, who stared angrily at the screen. "Do you think it's due to the servers frying? Maybe that knocked the computer back to the stone age?"

Yeni reached slowly toward the 3D screen, his finger shaking as he went to touch the curser. As his finger came close, a message began to resolve.

I see you...

Everyone thrust out of their chairs and their leader gestured wildly over his head. "Pack it up and destroy it all. You know the drill. We head out to the meeting spot and no one talk to anyone other than your partner on the street. Watch your back when you roll to the safe house. Make sure nobody follows you."

They had all freaked out by this point but did their best to get it together. As a methodical team, they grabbed the wires on the backs of each computer and yanked them from the sockets. One of the men walked down the line behind them to check every single server and every single plug. Everyone else collected any paperwork they had and disposed of it exactly as they were meant to. Yeni pushed them toward the doors and nodded to Hoff at the front.

He looked around one last time to ensure that the crew had removed all evidence from the place. At his shrill whistle, they raced toward the door, slammed it open, and barreled out of it. They scattered in different directions. Yeni stood in the doorway and fumed as he stared at the computer where the cursor still flashed on the screen. He flinched and gritted his teeth as flames blasted from the tables, traveled down the lines of electronics, and spilled over the floor.

The last of the hackers hurried over and slung his book bag on. Yeni slapped his back and shoved him out the door. He was pissed—beyond pissed, actually—but there it was, all his work ended in flames and shame. There hadn't been a gig like that in a long time, and he would have to tell the boss they couldn't handle it and left thousands of dollars of equipment to burn to cinders in the small house.

He turned and slammed the large metal door to trap the fire inside. As he walked, he flipped his hood up and stuck his hands into his pockets. Rain drizzled over his head and his boots splashed through the puddles that collected in the cracks and hollows of the pavement. He glanced back at the shimmer of the fire through the windows and wondered who the hell that guy was. They had done everything they were supposed to do, down to the last-second emergency pack-up. But there was someone out there who had made it his business to spook them.

The birds squawked as they flew high over the city. In the distance, the remnants of the old Eiffel Tower still sprawled in a pile where it had tumbled to ruin decades before. Buildings were patched and reworked, and from the rubble of the city, a new and more modern one had been born. Almost everyone who was currently alive had never even seen Paris before the destruction.

A long black limo pulled up in front of the looming skyscraper covered in shimmering glass. The driver walked around to the passenger side and opened the door, then stepped back. A long, muscular yet feminine, stocking-covered leg stepped out and planted the six-inch spiked heel of a stiletto on the asphalt. The woman inside squinted, donned her large-rimmed sunglasses, and ducked out of the vehicle. She tugged nonchalantly on her skirt and tucked her clutch under her arm. Tall and well built, she possessed the perfect amount of curve coupled with strong, lean muscles.

She stepped up on the curb and ran her black-leather-gloved hand down the back of her short red hair. As she took a deep breath, she pursed her lips and glanced up the side of the monster building. "It seems they are doing well here."

The driver wiggled his brow and closed the car door and she walked through the courtyard out front past a fountain that had no water in it. As she approached the door, a tall, dark-skinned man dressed in a black suit, white shirt, and black tie, opened it for her. She could see the gun tucked snugly in the side of his pants as she passed. Everyone carried weapons these days.

As she entered the lobby of the building, she removed her glasses and glanced around. It was decorated with large paintings, plush throw rugs, and fake plants, much like any other office. In the corner was the elevator so she hurried over and stepped inside. She took a keycard from her purse, slid it into the slot, and pressed the fifteenth-floor button. The doors shut and the elevator began to ascend.

There were no stops taken on the way, and when it reached the destination, she had to remove her card for the doors to open. The elevator dinged to notify the people in the office that someone had arrived. There were no full-time office companies in the building. It was, instead, a place where temporary corporate headquarters were constructed in secret and with anonymity.

The secretary at the desk put her pen down and smiled sweetly. "How can I help you today?"

The woman looked at her for a moment and flipped her elevator keycard over to reveal a symbol on the back. The secretary's face didn't change. She nodded and picked the phone up. The visitor glanced around the plush office and decided it could be called almost comfortable. These types of places were hired locations for companies around the world, and she assumed they had to be as nice as possible.

They weren't that expensive, not compared to some of the rents that companies often paid to be in the center of the rich communities. At the same time, though, it wasn't breaking-the-bank expensive either. There was a moderation to it that kept it healthy for them and everyone else who used the facility. Not to mention the fact that the view from the identical sides of the building was absolutely amazing. It was unlike any of the other ones she had been in.

Her gaze flickered across a large mirror in the small sitting area. Her stark white skirt fell to her knees and her jacket was perfectly tailored. The light pink blouse was modest but unbuttoned possibly one button too low. She was educated and possessed an intelligence beyond that of almost everyone she ever really found herself around. Confidence was something she didn't lack in the least. It was, in fact, something she had in spades.

That assertiveness was reflected in her walk. Her steps, although governed by the stilettos, were decisive and brisk. She always placed the heel of her shoe down first and tapped down with the toe and had walked in them long enough that there wasn't even a slight wiggle in her ankle. But with them on, she moved with stealth and assurance and her strides matched the situation and placed her firmly in control.

Her gaze flickered around her and hesitated on the man who sat in the corner with a newspaper. He studied her body as she walked and gave him the impression of a circling tiger—aware of her surroundings but sleek and smooth in movement.

The man's gaze met hers and she smiled at him, which immediately and somewhat surprisingly lowered his anxiety. She had perfectly straight bleached teeth and the red lipstick contrasted severely. Her eyes were narrowed and dangerous-looking but when she smiled, that went away to be replaced by a twinkle in her eye that caused some reactions from those who milled about the offices. It took them off guard and they either immediately diverted their gazes or smiled back awkwardly with uncertainty.

The secretary stopped, removed a key from around her neck, inserted it in the door, and opened it. "Right this way."

The woman nodded with a smile and walked into the conference room. A buffet-style mahogany table stretched along the back wall and a large, oval-shaped one in the middle would seat six comfortably.

The secretary hovered in the doorway, her hands clasped together in front of her. "There are Danishes, small sandwiches, and cookies on the table. There is coffee brewing if you would like it that way. Otherwise, I can secure you any type of stimulant that you might need. We know not everyone maintains their energy in the same way."

"No, coffee will be fine," she replied. "I'll fix it myself."

The woman crossed to the center table and sat on one side. The secretary bowed slightly and left, closing the door quickly behind her. The woman put her hands on the table and folded them together to enjoy the silence of the room but without the nerves anyone else might have in that moment.

Suddenly, a crackling noise intruded, and a male voice echoed from the speakers of the phone in front of her. "Welcome, Ms. Elizabeth."

Her gaze shifted to the device and she leaned back. No video displayed on the screen, only audio. The small button on top flickered green to confirm that the line was, in fact, in use and secure. The monitor flickered slightly, and the ONE R&D logo appeared. It turned and twisted, rose in 3D fashion from the screen, and floated in front of her. She was indeed in the right place and oddly, it seemed even more secretive than she would have assumed it would be. That she was familiar with, though. She had dealt with the quiet back-alley approach to business for her entire career.

The voice was steady with no sound of breathing or movement. Silence now ensued, waiting for the woman to respond to the greeting. Still, she was slightly hesitant and knew exactly why she felt that way.

She narrowed her eyes and leaned forward to speak into the phone. "I didn't provide you with that name."

There was no response for several moments and then the voice spoke once more. "We are an R&D company, Ms. Elizabeth. If we were incapable of even researching the name of the woman we invited into our private offices, we wouldn't stay in business for very long, now would we?"

The side of her mouth tugged into a smile. "No, I suppose not. Although that constitutes more than a simple Internet search in order to find that information. But I will be impressed then, rather than angry."

"Ah, very good. We don't want to start this off on the wrong foot, now do we? I believe that you will make a perfect addition to the set of plans I am currently putting together for a very large undertaking."

She crossed her legs, her eyes narrowed and her lips pursed, and instantly understood what was happening there. "I wondered, at first, as to why you wanted to talk to me. I guess I shouldn't be shocked."

Ms. Elizabeth leaned back and decided to wait a while before she made her coffee. "I am under the assumption that if I turned the phone off, you would still be able to contact me. Through the television, the lines around us, the reception from the building across the street. Even the faintest of signals."

The voice was silent for a moment. "Very good, Ms. Elizabeth. You are as quick as they tell me you are."

She chuckled and shook her head. "Okay, you want to talk? Let's talk. You have my full attention."

Her father tapped on the top of the roof inside their car. "AI, no need to park in the spots. You can let us out on the curb. We would like to say goodbye."

The AI replied and its voice broke slightly, much like the one in the security system at home. "Of course, Mr. Morgan. May I wish you safe journeys, Stephanie."

She smiled as the car came to a stop. "Thank you, Mildred. You have safe travels as well."

They all piled out in front of the TRAM station. She had the car she could have used, but her parents insisted that they drop her off on their way to work. She stood, one hand on her unbraided hair, and the wide legs of her high-waisted black pants flapped in the breeze. As part of the outfit, she wore a short, cap-sleeved white button-up with small ruffles down the front. She had even applied a little makeup, trying out her abilities with what she already had.

Her father gave her a hug. "Remember, hands behind you or in your lap. As far as your discussions go, show manners, of course, but remember, they are courting you as much as you are them. Don't be a pushover."

She nodded. "Of course. Thank you."

He fiddled in his back pocket, retrieved something small wrapped in a piece of cloth, and put it quickly in her hand. "I would give you some sort of advice on protection, but I think that may be all you need."

She lifted the fabric to find a battery beneath it. He nodded. "I think you can protect yourself. That's simply a little a protection in a bottle from your old worried dad. If you need to use it, make sure they stay down."

While he gave his daughter a wink, Cindy stood there with a stern face, her jaw clenched and arms folded. She was not amused by his antics in the least. Still, Stephanie clutched the battery in her hand and held it slightly behind her so her mother wouldn't take it.

Cindy walked up and brushed her daughter's hair off her shoulders. "Don't listen to your father. He only wants to see that you've kicked ass and taken names. Don't give in to his fantasies and indulge his masculinity. Be safe, let us know you have arrived, and we will see you when you get back."

Stephanie gave them another hug and kiss goodbye and chuckled as her mom squeezed her super tight. She still acted like she was leaving for the first time ever, although she didn't really mind. What mattered was that she knew they loved her and she knew that she was lucky to have that. As she lifted her suitcase, she glanced back. Her mother walked ahead of her dad, who looked back at her as well. He grinned and she winked at him with a smile and dropped the battery into her pocket.

She hurried with her bag to the boarding area and retrieved her ticket. The collector, a tall chubby man with a stern face, grabbed it from her and read the print. She watched as his face softened quickly and he snapped his fingers. A bell boy of sorts hurried up, his hat slightly cocked to the side.

The collector looked at him with disapproval. "Take Ms. Morgana's bag and escort her to train car three. Anything you need, madam, Jeffrey here will be happy to secure for you."

Stephanie smirked. "Thank you, sir."

The kid showed her to a ramp specially placed for first-class passengers. They had even draped the rigid metal with a red carpet. She walked gingerly up it and stood inside, waiting for the kid with her suitcase. He nodded nervously, adjusted his hat, and led her quickly through a very fancy dining car. White linens were draped on each table beneath small bunches of flowers in vases and china set for each place.

She swallowed hard and glanced at the different forks and knives. Ironically, she would have to rely on the little training she had in manners at the prep school because this would be the first time she had ever been a guest in such opulence. They walked through the tunnel into the next car and the attendant stopped outside an enclosed room with etched glass doors. He opened the door for her and lowered his gaze to the floor.

Stephanie smiled and tried not to giggle or snort in her nervousness. She stepped into the car and immediately glanced up at a small crystal chandelier that hung from the ceiling. Inside the small room, four reclining overstuffed chairs with wooden tips on the arms were neatly arranged. All were empty but one, and when she saw who the man was—or rather, what he was— her heart skipped a beat.

There was no mistaking the pale, almost sparkling skin, long pointed ears, and billowing hair. He was a Meligornian dressed in Earth clothing and he stared out of the window as the train prepared to move. She hesitated for a moment, glanced at the kid, and stepped inside. The boy hurried in and placed her suitcase in the luggage closet, then strapped it to the shelf to avoid it shifting and injuring anyone. He closed the large doors quietly and his gaze wandered nervously to the Meligornian symbol on the shoulder of the man's suit.

While the nerves rippled hastily through her, Stephanie quietly took a deep breath and released it slowly. *Pull it together, Stephanie. This is no different than any of the times inside the Virtual World with the Meligornians you have met before. He is only a magical being.*

She didn't know this, of course, but her closed cabin with the Meligornian was set up by none other than BURT. Quietly, she took her seat, linked her hands in her lap, and tried to keep her attention focused out the window. Before the TRAM began to move, there was a loud knock on the door and what looked like an enormous bodyguard ducked in and glanced darkly at her for several moments. It made the hair on the back of her neck stand up.

CHAPTER NINETEEN

The train powered along at high speed, but the windows still displayed a leisurely pace that allowed for a pleasant view over the countryside. The car was quiet—definitely much quieter than their trip last time, although Stephanie was sure she had read something about sound dampening technology used in the first-class areas of the TRAMs. At the time, she hadn't given it a second thought, but now, speeding along yet feeling as if she was seated comfortably in her living room felt almost ridiculous.

Her gaze moved to the Meligornian and she noticed that he wore the metal of the Meligorn Government. From the way he was dressed to the symbols on his shoulders and sleeves, she could assume that he was high up in the government, too. How high she wasn't sure, but she decided that if they allowed her in there too, it couldn't have been very high. Everything in her wanted to strike up a conversation with him. If he was a government official, she wanted to know about that, how they worked as a civilization, and all the things in between. But at the same time, she didn't want to act like a ridiculous fangirl.

She wrinkled her nose and turned her head back toward the windows as they entered their first stretch of the TRAM tunnel.

A screen darkened on the windows to shut out the unsightly concrete walls and water stains and the lights in the cabin brightened somewhat. As she glanced down from the ceiling, the Meligornian looked at her with curious eyes.

Stephanie felt awkward and didn't hold his gaze. His bodyguard had taken the seat beside him and the two had their phones out in their laps. It was obvious that they wanted to have a private conversation from the fact that they seemed to have been texting each other.

The ambassador looked at the screen on his phone and read the message from his bodyguard. **I trust you will discuss this security breach with the humans when you reach DC, Ambassador V'ritan?**

He sighed but without rancor. **She is only a girl, and in fact, there is something about her that I can't help but feel that I recognize.**

The guard raised an eyebrow. **I don't see how that is possible, but I will do the research really fast.**

The ambassador put his phone in his pocket and turned his attention to the tablet in his lap before he sighed again and stared at the tip of his shiny shoes. After a few moments, a dinging sounded and the guard nodded. "Just a reminder of the trip. Although I suppose I put the time in wrong again."

Stephanie didn't even look at them. The ambassador picked his tablet up and flipped through his notes for his upcoming meetings. A number of them had been scheduled over the next several days and he had tried his utmost to prepare for such a busy time. Meligornians on the home planet did not stress their bodies like that, but after so many years on Earth, he was used to the high-paced lifestyle. He merely wished he had more time to memorize all the statistics. The notes were firmly lodged in his head, but the numbers gave him grief. Whether the humans thought it was debatable or not, math did not turn out to be the language of all living creatures.

Nonetheless, he prepared his notes in a way that they could understand. He went to flip another page and paused when his guard stiffened beside him. Hastily, he glanced up to see if the girl had seen it, but she had not. She stared at a book in her lap and obviously tried to make things not so awkward inside the train car.

As he looked at his notes again, a warning symbol from his bodyguard appeared on his screen. He moved it away and clicked on the link that he had sent. It was newspaper clippings of the girl across from them that reported how she was the first Earth witch ever to be discovered. They included pictures of her walking with friends and family and other images of her shooting blue streams of energy. Curiously, her eyes glistened in that same color.

He found it slightly amusing that she walked around so nonchalantly and tried not to be noticed. The bodyguard sent another few articles to him and he crossed his leg and tilted the tablet slightly to take advantage of better lighting. He began to read through each one carefully, but all of them said almost the same thing. She had thrown magic to help save a woman and her child. Some hailed her as an angel and a savior, while others were terrified of this new evolutionary—or perhaps revolutionary— manifestation of power.

As he skimmed through, he glanced at her from time to time. He noticed her hand in her pocket that seemed to roll something around in it nervously. He could only assume that it was one of her magic batteries. It didn't give him pause, though. To him, there was nothing dangerous about her. At least there wouldn't be when she faced a Meligornian.

His guard rested his hand casually on his gun. The ambassador clicked his tongue and shook his head to remind him to take it easy. With another glance at the girl, he wondered how much of his language she could speak.

After a few moments during which she knew he was staring

while he struggled to find the right words, he finally decided to speak to her. *"K'roth gurardian brofton nationalie* Capitol?"

She blinked for a moment and looked up slowly.

The Russian delegate slammed his fist down on the table, stood, and leaned forward on it. "You think that because NorAm killed the Russian dictator hundreds of years ago that gives you the right to give me any shit about this? We have reinstated our country, while you sat around bathing in luxury and waste with these rich people."

The American narrowed his eyes and pointed at him. "Now you hold on right there. How do you have the nerve to talk about us in that manner? That is beyond treasonous with your stories of hate for people who would drive you to separate from the idea that the Federation worked so desperately to get you on. And then to turn around and rob one of our American banks."

The Russian clenched his fist and yelled at the American, "Regardless of the crime, your assault on Russian citizens and the danger you put all of them in is tantamount to war. We have fought wars for less and trust me, everyone outside the Federation has been dying to see NorAm have their asses beaten. You are arrogant and uncareful as you speak to the great leaders of this world. You are the country that allowed this plastic lifestyle everyone so dutifully clings to and we are the ones who stepped above you, not interested in being under the thumb of the Federation."

The Chinese delegate waved his hand and scoffed. "You fight over nothing. We are the ones who are the true victims here."

Both the Russians and the Americans went quiet and looked curiously at him. The Chinese delegate's forehead was furrowed, and he spoke with passion as he waved his fist up and down. "You have the nerve to touch our sovereignty. You both used your abilities through your own countries to do so. You have broken treaties and understandings between our countries. While you Americans believe that because you fall under Federation protection, you can do anything that you want, you are wrong. So very wrong. And you Russians, with your talk of war. You have no leg to stand on. If anyone here should be threatening, it should be China. We are fed up with this."

The American delegate shook his head. "We are doing no such thing. If we had the power to do anything we wanted, we would have used it on your asses already."

The meeting came to a standstill and all three delegates finally resumed their seats. They remained quiet for several minutes until they were able to calm themselves enough to discuss what had happened. There was actually no real evidence to confirm that any of them had officially been involved. They had all simply made assumptions because they knew the suspected hackers had come into the United States from Russia.

After a few moments, the American delegate cleared his throat and gestured to his Chinese counterpart. "I thought it was you guys all pissed off at us. We figured you had reason with the trade issues and conversations with the Federation and the poverty your country has fallen into due to the lack of resources available. I am sorry. I am a professional. I should not jump to conclusions."

The Chinese man calmed himself as well. The delegate leaned forward toward the mic. "We appreciate your apology and accept. In all honesty, our country assumed it was Russia that had egged things on and made it impossible for you to respect our sovereignty and go after them in the same arena."

The Russian delegate shook his head. "If it was none of us, then who was it?"

They all swallowed and thought the same thing. The three major players—as well as many of the smaller countries—had all experienced some degree of cybersecurity alarms on the fateful day in question. While they had all immediately put their best counter-hackers and analysts to work, no one seemed to be able to determine the real origin of either the initial attack or the swift and decisive counterstrikes that had drawn all nations into the arena. The clean-up had been so swift and so efficiently executed that there was no way to unravel the source or correctly determine how many counter-specialists had been involved.

If the truth be told, their best and most experienced cyber teams were baffled, and from there, it had been easy to slide into the vague and murky waters of paranoia and fearful assumptions. More than anything, all members present wanted answers—at the very least, an explanation of what exactly had happened. The truth that stared them in the face in that moment was one none of them wanted, or ever expected, to face.

There could very well be a country out there that had hidden their abilities. A country that was more powerful and skillful than all of them.

Stephanie swallowed hard as her eyes widened and her palms sweated. She was astonished to be addressed in Meligornian and although she didn't speak it, she was very honored that he would even speak to her. Also, this was no avatar, so she knew she had to be very polite. It was no simulation within the Virtual World. This was real.

She stood carefully and bowed, raised one hand up, and extended the other out for his. While she wasn't sure if he was on the cusp of the royal greeting or not, she decided that something was better than nothing. She not only wanted to show her admiration and respect for the Meligornian people but also to show her excitement at the opportunity to ride the train with someone of his stature.

The bodyguard maintained a stiff expression, but as the

ambassador stood and walked toward her, his mouth dropped open. The official bowed his head, raised his hand, and grasped her forearm with the other. They both held the greeting for several moments to show suitable reverence before they gave each other the traditional Meligornian verbal greeting.

As Stephanie straightened, her cheeks flushed and her excitement grew within her. But she knew that if she couldn't understand him, it would be no good anyway. She thought back to that lesson and smiled, placed her hands behind her back, and latched onto her wrists. "Engotish Preferatus Ingorna Discusio?"

The ambassador cracked a smile and raised his eyebrows at the guard. He looked at her again as they took their seats. "Of course we can."

She looked around as giddiness bubbled to the surface. "But you didn't do a cantrip or spell or anything."

He chuckled. "When you reach my age of over two hundred years old, you tend to be able to achieve the required results without even opening your mouth."

Stephanie bit the inside of her lip and tapped her fingers on her knees as she sat on the edge of the seat. Finally, it got the better of her, and she burst into a smile. "I'm sorry. This is so awesome—to get to ride with a real Meligornian, that is. I have only met one in my VR studies, never in real life. I didn't know if I actually ever would."

The guard watched her as she giggled and shook her head, apparently on the verge of talking excitedly to herself. A smile moved across his lips as it did for the ambassador as well. They both realized quickly that she was no threat to anyone. She was merely a curious young adult with a heart that seemed to be true.

The ambassador motioned to the guard and said something in his ear. The man nodded and stood, walked across, and extended his hand to Stephanie. She looked at him nervously for a moment and he chuckled. "He would like you to join him."

She smiled and took his hand, scooted past him, and sat

beside the ambassador. They sat there talking and paid little attention to the rising and setting sun displayed in the glass windows. They learned language nuances like what awesome meant and the fact that he had asked her originally if she was the human who knew magic.

In the progression of the discussion, without even knowing it was happening, Stephanie began to ask questions of a high-level wizard—the kind of questions that only a theorist would have asked. The ambassador, having had many, many years of practice in maintaining a collected state of being, did not flinch or spark a notion that he was indeed shocked that she could be human and have that level of Meligornian experience.

Curious, he began to probe her knowledge. "And you have tried to concentrate the magic within you to carry it?"

Stephanie nodded. "I have. And it has worked for a few moments but when my thoughts change, I lose it. However, I am currently working on a theory that if I pull it into an imagined object in my thoughts, I will be able to secure it and siphon from it as needed."

The ambassador rubbed his chin. "That is an interesting theory but one thing you have not accounted for is the strain that it will have on the human mind. Meligornian magic and energy has its own flow—a soul, almost, if you will. The connection to that energy must be there to avoid any type of negative consequence."

She nodded and her eyes remained fixed on the floor. "That makes sense. If I try to force it, it will only reject me, just as we have rejected its pull on Earth for so long. Like those who can't feel it at all."

The ambassador smiled. "Those who cannot sense the energy are more than merely mentally blocked. They do not possess the inner strength that is passed through the universe. We do not know how humans have acquired it but for everyone but you, apparently, it is only strong enough to feel."

Stephanie was having the time of her life. The Meligornian official had helped her understand theories that she had not even known were different than what she thought. It made a lot of difference when it came to working with the magic.

They continued their conversation without realizing that they were so close to their destination. Before they knew it, the train had pulled into the station in DC. The ambassador walked her out, and they shared a traditional Meligornian goodbye. She began to walk away, carrying her bag in a complete haze.

"Ms. Morgana," the Meligornian called to her. "Wait one minute."

CHAPTER TWENTY

Stephanie turned, her eyes wide, and smiled as the guard lumbered toward her with something in his hand. He was a large man—a human—and although he gave the appearance of pure muscle, she could tell he had grown a little soft with age. She estimated him to be nearing forty or so, but the creases at the corners of his eyes showed that he had been in that job for quite some time. There was a protectiveness but also a kindness in him that made her feel safe.

He handed a small white card to her. "Keep this to yourself."

She took it in her left hand and nodded as she reached her right out to shake. He smiled widely and gripped her hand gently, almost able to wrap his entire fist around her dainty fingers and palm. He glanced over his shoulder and laughed a little harder as he shook his head. "I have been with him for a very long time. I have to admit, he hasn't had this much fun in years. It is nice to see him enjoy himself. That is something his job does not allow very often. Thank you, young Stephanie. Be safe."

Stephanie shook her head with a bemused grin and watched as he walked away. She looked at the special card in her hand and chewed on her bottom lip. She had read about these cards on the

Meligorn Magical Musings website. After a moment's hesitation, she slid her hand into her pocket and clasped the battery, applying the smallest amount of magic she could. The card seemed to shiver in her fingertips and his information, written in white on the white background, vibrated. She watched in wonder as it lifted off the card and floated toward her.

It seemed almost alive as it found its way to her forehead and pressed against it. The information glowed for a moment before it faded into her mind. She blinked her eyes and focused on the image of his phone number in her head as if she actually read it on a piece of paper. There was no other time that she could think of that her thoughts had been that completely clear. It was almost magical in itself how well it worked.

She released the battery and turned her attention to the now blank piece of stock card in her palm. It began to disintegrate and churn into a fine dust in the center of her hand. When she tilted her hand from side to side, the ash shimmered in the light. A small breeze blew, swept the ash up, and carried it away. Stephanie giggled as she stood there and watched the dance of the wind. When the last of the sparkle had disappeared into the clouds above, she sighed, a contented grin on her cheeks.

Ambassador V'ritan smiled and rubbed his hands together. He'd watched her face, seen that she had almost immediately known what to do with the card and then, without thought, simply did it. She showed ingenuity and bravery in that moment, something he didn't find in very many humans. In fact, those qualities weren't always present in every Meligornian he met, either. Like humans, the Meligornians had their fair share of those who worked outside of the parameters of what was expected of them. The difference was that the humans had evolved to know how to handle that, while those in Meligorn with that distinct inability to regulate usually ended up dying tragically in some battle on the planet.

He took a deep breath and turned to his guard. "Brilgus?"

His bodyguard, who was collecting the luggage, stopped to listen. "Yes, Ambassador?"

"I would like her followed," he replied. "I want to know what she is doing here in this city, especially on her own. It is not the place you would suggest a human-born magi would choose to wander around in. What she has not fully come to understand is that humans have a fear of what they do not understand, while Meligornians tend to have a curiosity until burned. What is different, as we saw when we first came to this planet, is considered a threat to their kind."

Brilgus waved at one of the other guards who had been present on the TRAM but remained at a discreet distance. "The ambassador would like a tail on her. Nothing too close as to alert her that we are watching but you are to keep a close eye and report back when any new information presents itself."

V'ritan put up his hand. "No, Brilgus, I would like you to handle this one. I trust you to keep her safe—and to ensure that you are not discovered. Should you have to make yourself known for any critical reason, she will more readily trust you rather than a stranger. My concerns may be groundless, of course, and I certainly hope they are. But these humans don't know what they have. They haven't yet discovered the rarity and importance of someone of her kind. It would be a shame for the fire to go out too early. And we know exactly what happens to those who stand up to the Federation."

Brilgus nodded. "They are extinguished."

The ambassador nodded slowly, his eyes fixed on her retreating figure. "Yes, Brilgus, they are extinguished. Thank you for doing this. I know it is outside of your normal commands. And I think it would be best if we kept it between us for the moment. Until I learn more about what is going on, of course."

The guard bowed his head. "Of course. Anything that you think is right."

Tearing his eyes away from her, the ambassador patted him

on the shoulder with a smile. "Go on. Don't let her get away from you. She is younger, smaller, and nimbler. We don't want you to have to stay at a job the whole time—you might fall out with that amount of muscle on your bones."

Brilgus rolled his eyes. "This is pure steel. You should feel lucky to have me protecting you."

V'ritan laughed. "As I do. Very lucky. And now, she can too."

The guard frowned, turned, and followed as nonchalantly as he could as she pushed through the crowd and out to where the cars were parked, waiting for the passengers to emerge.

***

Stephanie released a deep breath as she set her heavy case down and retrieved her instructions. "There should be a car here for me somewhere."

She scanned the self-driving cars and at the scrolling signs on the top for any sign of her name. Infuriatingly, she didn't see it anywhere.

"Excuse me, but are you Ms. Morgana?" a voice asked from beside her.

She turned to find an older gentleman dressed in a driver's coat with the collar high on his neck and split slightly in the front. His black pants were perfectly pressed, and the tips of his shoes shone brightly. His driver's hat fit his head perfectly as if it were created for no one but him. "I am Stephanie Morgana, yes."

He smiled and leaned down to pick up her bag. "Right this way."

She glanced around before she followed him, and her mouth dropped open as he opened the back passenger door to a distinguished black limousine. After a moment, she laughed and hurried forward and thanked her driver as she ducked in and he closed the door behind her. The lights were dim inside, but the floor and the ceiling lit up and it seemed as if there were fish tanks above and below her. A droid hovered over a small bar to the right.

Without a doubt, she was definitely impressed. The ride was so smooth that she barely even knew they were moving. The droid poured her a soda by request and rested on its charging base. Before long, the driver opened the door for her again, this time welcoming her to the Plaza del Infinito, one of the most exclusive hotels in Washington DC. She knew that because she had seen the pictures of the rooftop pool when she had researched the capital.

As she walked toward the entrance to the beautiful hotel, she couldn't help but wonder why she had been given this kind of treatment—the kind she imagined the Meligornian official would receive, not some kid from the Chicago Gov-Subs who happened to know how to throw magic. Almost as soon as that thought entered her mind, the training she had received throughout her life kicked into high gear. It was almost like a swift kick in her ass.

There was no reason that she should feel not good enough to have that kind of lifestyle. Or, for that matter, why she should feel uncomfortable walking into that hotel and across the glistening white marble floors and the projected ceiling that created a moving face. When she looked closer, the face changed, mimicking the past presidents of the country.

You need to value yourself more than other people do. Even more than this company seems to be doing.

Stephanie pep-talked herself as she walked along. She wouldn't allow herself to make the same mistake that ignorance so easily caused. The sound of a sweet, kind voice shook her from her thoughts, and she looked up to find that she now stood at the desk, having been too deep in her thoughts to notice. The woman behind the counter wore a hip-length jacket that clipped tightly in the front, was perfectly pressed, and had gold bands around the sleeves.

Her bright blonde hair was tied back in a sensible bun and her blue eyes sparkled. "How can I help you today?"

She retrieved her piece of paper. "I'm Stephanie Morgana. I should have a reservation."

The clerk looked through the system and smiled as she handed the note back and removed a golden key from a drawer in front of her. She then picked up the phone and pressed only one key. "Yes, our Gold Standard customer has arrived. Excellent."

She hung up and looked at the girl. "Our concierge Albert is on his way to show you the grounds and your room. In the meantime, please press your palm to the reader so we can register you."

Stephanie nodded. "Okay. Thank you." She complied with the request and it only took a moment before the light clicked to green to confirm success.

The woman opened a small folder and went down the list on the right to explain the amenities. "Coffee maker, one cup or full, you can choose. There is a steamer for your clothes, but if you would prefer, you can send them down here and we can do it. We would only need a couple of minutes to get them done. Breakfast will be brought to you and there is an AI service in your suite that you can speak to about a wakeup call. To change the scenery in your room, ask the AI to jostle the walls and she will walk you through it. If you have any questions, there is an earpiece in a case on the nightstand. You can put it in and press the small button on the side. It will ring through here and we will be happy to help."

Albert walked up. "Hello, Ms. Morgana. May I take your bag and show you to your room?"

Stephanie smiled and handed him her suitcase. She felt weird not carrying it herself, but she shrugged the discomfort off as they walked down the hall to a bank of elevators. Her instinct had been to stop there but Albert continued to the end of the hall and a shimmering golden elevator.

She stepped up beside him and he nodded at the palm scan. She pressed her hand to it, and the bell tolled before the doors slid open. As they stepped into the elevator, she turned to him. "I heard there is a pool on the roof?"

Albert smiled, his hands behind him. "Yes, but you have your own mini pool inside the suite. You were booked for the Elite Royal. There are three bedrooms, a study, the pool room, and a living room."

Stephanie blinked as the elevator opened into the huge apartment at the top of the building. "What would I possibly need with all this space?"

Albert chuckled and walked through to set her bag down in what she assumed was a bedroom. "Will you need anything else?"

Stephanie fumbled in her pocket and pulled out some gold Federation dollars. "No thank you, but here, it's the best I have."

Albert smiled kindly. "My gratuity, as well as everyone else's, has been taken care of."

He left in the elevator and Stephanie wandered through the vibrant apartment and into the first bedroom on the right in search of her suitcase. She stared at the huge king-sized bed for a moment but gasped as she looked beyond it. The walls were all made of glass and provided a breathtaking view of the crystal blue water of the Maldives. It was, she recalled learning, virtually the only place left on Earth that was lush and full of life.

"Welcome to your suite, Ms. Morgana," the AI's voice said crisply. "How can I be of service?"

Stephanie found her suitcase on the luggage rack. "I'll unpack my suitcase, but do I have a television in here?"

"Of course," the AI replied and immediately transformed one wall of the room to a giant television. "Is this satisfactory?"

She stared at it in disbelief for a moment. "Yep. That will do it."

The news was on and she let it play in the background as she unpacked quickly. She half listened as they talked about a Dreth pirate raid that had killed an entire fleet of Federation soldiers in deep space. It was something that happened often.

The news anchor continued, her voice muffled in the background of her thoughts. "….Meligorn…"

Stephanie stopped and whirled toward the television. "Volume higher."

The volume increased immediately. "In international news, the Meligorn High Council Special Envoy and Ambassador to the King of Meligorn arrived in Washington DC today. It is his first trip back to the city in nearly three months. He is here to meet with the world leaders about the Dreth pirate crisis as well as other Federation concerns."

Stephanie put her hands to her cheeks as the news played footage of him getting into a limo and waving to the crowd. "Oh, my God, that was not a high wizard on the TRAM! That was… that was… his majesty's Special Envoy High Ambassador."

For several moments, she freaked, completely in heaven at having met and talked to someone so important. But it wasn't long before the information began to sink in. "Oh, shit! I didn't bow correctly. He gets a royal greeting. I touched him when I wasn't supposed to ever touch a royal."

She dropped her hands to her side in horror, but common sense kicked in and she smiled. There was no way she could have known. But now, she couldn't believe that she had spoken to one of the highest of the high on Meligorn.

"Awesome," she whispered before she turned her attention back to her clothes.

Stephanie hung them all in the closet and the AI showed her how it acted as a steamer for wrinkles as well as giving them a scent. She chose morning lilac because it was her mom's favorite.

"What should I call you?" she asked as she looked around.

The AI paused. "You can call me Sarah."

She nodded cheerfully. "Perfect. Sarah, I'm so hungry but I don't want to go out."

"Then let me run you through the room service menu," she replied and pulled it up on the wall Stephanie happened to be facing.

Dinner was absolutely amazing that night. Stephanie sat in a big fluffy robe while a droid did her toenails, and enjoyed an absolutely delicious dessert to celebrate the craziness that everything had become. She figured she deserved to take advantage of what was offered. Even if the job paid enough for her to live that way, she knew she wouldn't. She would still be her, only she would get her mom and dad out of the Gov-Subs and set them up for the rest of their lives. But why not enjoy it for a couple of days?

"Sarah, can you call my mom?"

The AI dinged. "Pairing with tablet…calling Mom."

The wall lit up with a telephone symbol as it rang. Suddenly, her mother appeared, looking like a giant version of herself. "Hi, honey!"

Stephanie giggled. "Hi, Mom!"

"Wow, are you using the hotel phone? It has a great camera angle."

She nodded and kicked her feet. "You are literally talking to me from one whole wall. This place is crazy."

Cindy was wowed. "That sounds so cool. So, it's a good place? Did you eat?"

"Did I ever." Stephanie rubbed her belly. "I had filet mignon, potatoes with cheese and some sort of oil they called truffle. Then I had Meligorn baked pombos, which are similar to apples, but sweeter."

Her mother's eyes widened. "Wow. That sounds delicious. I should have stowed away in your suitcase."

Stephanie turned to lie on her stomach on the bed and kicked her feet behind her. "That would have been so much fun. And you would have died on the TRAM. I was put in a first-class cabin and there was one other person in there. He was a Meligornian and I thought the whole time that I was talking to a high wizard."

Cindy raised an eyebrow. "Who was he?"

Stephanie snorted. "Only the Special Envoy High Ambassador."

Her mom's mouth dropped open. "Good God. What was he like? Was he nice?"

"Oh, man, was he ever," she gushed. "He taught me all kinds of things and gave me his number in case I needed anything while I was here. It was really so crazy."

Cindy wrinkled her nose and smiled. "I'm so glad. You deserve all of this, you know that, right? You are an amazing woman, and this is special for you."

"Thanks, Mom," Stephanie said sweetly as she yawned. "Oh, man, I'm exhausted."

"I bet. Meeting royalty, eating meat that I have never had a taste of, and now this hotel. You need to have some rest. It's a big day tomorrow. And I have to pick up your father. He stayed behind to fix something at the shop. He will never just rest."

Stephanie sat up and wiped her eyes, the sleeves of her robe way too long. "Okay. Tell Daddy I love him. And I'll let you know how everything goes."

Cindy blew her a big kiss. "Will do, baby. See you soon."

The wall went dark and Stephanie yawned again. The AI sensed her mood and immediately dimmed the lights and turned the walls and the ceiling into celestial scenes of swirling heavenly bodies. Sounds of calm and peace played quietly overhead as she curled up in the middle of the huge bed, pulled the down comforter over her, and fell asleep almost instantly.

CHAPTER TWENTY-ONE

The next morning, Sarah woke her with gentle morning lights and sweet harmonic music. Inside the bathroom was an entire shower room rather than a stall or bathtub. The water fell from the ceiling like a gentle waterfall and steam warmed the entire room. She was so caught up in the luxury that she had to basically run downstairs to reach the car on time.

The limo was waiting for her and they headed out to the east side of the city. Her nerves kicked in as soon as she settled into the limo, and even though the old capital was right outside, she couldn't focus on it at all. When they pulled up to their destination, Stephanie was slightly disappointed. Compared to the luxury she had recently left, the place looked run-down. It was in a warehouse park with a guard shack out front and not much of anything else.

The truth was that BURT had been so caught up in all the other details and wanted a place that wouldn't draw attention, so he hadn't put much thought into the outside appearance. The car drove through and pulled up at the front of the building. The driver opened her door and helped her out. She smoothed her navy-blue sleeveless dress and grabbed her envelope of information.

The driver stopped and nodded. "I will be back at 3:00 PM sharp to pick you up. I'll be right here."

Stephanie smiled and patted him on the shoulder, both as a show of thanks and to recover her resolve for the meeting and put on her professional face. At least, that's what she hoped it was. She headed to the front doors and blew out a breath before she yanked it open and walked inside. As soon as she stepped through the entryway, the lights brightened and revealed a desk in front of her. Lights shimmered as a virtual secretary appeared.

It was actually pretty cool. "Welcome, Stephanie Morgana, to ONE R&D. To get you set up to go, please step up to the counter and place your palms on the surface and look directly into the retinal scanner."

She stepped forward, placed her palms down, and smiled as it scanned her hands. The retinal scanner was fast and had already flashed green by the time she pulled her head back. The door opened to her right and Ms. Elizabeth walked through. She wore slim, fitted black slacks that ended at the ankles, a black belt, and a plain button-up white shirt tucked in. Her heels clicked as she walked forward.

Stephanie turned toward her and clutched her envelope tightly. Ms. Elizabeth put her hand out and shook hers. "Hello, Steph, my name is Elizabeth Smith. Why don't you come on back with me?"

She nodded nervously and walked past the woman and through the door. Elizabeth glared at the secretary. "No more visitors."

The holographic secretary nodded and clicked a virtual button to bolt the front doors.

BURT finished the upgrade to the Dreth multi-team battle a second or so before the notification came through that Stephanie had arrived at ONE R&D. He apportioned part of his focus to the meeting room and tested all the video and mics hastily to ensure that everything was hooked up properly. He had rented the building but installed everything he would need to observe digitally.

Stephanie sat at the table with a mug of coffee in her hand. Elizabeth popped a chocolate in her mouth and set the plate down on the table. "Chocolate? They are the best in DC."

She shrugged, took one, and definitely agreed once it was in her mouth. Elizabeth sat across from her and rested her elbows on the long, shiny black table. She laced her fingers together and waited for the girl to finish chewing. She played the role of a high-level executive, exactly the kind you would find at a facility like that. However, that was not even close to the kinds of roles she'd had in the past.

Elizabeth was what someone would call a Jack of all trades. Before coming to ONE R&D, she had been an operative for several private companies across the globe. She could essentially find, retrieve, and keep safe anyone or anything that someone needed and was willing to pay the big bucks for. After several years of that, though, she'd grown tired and entered into the consultation business for all security needs—from a small-time burglary system at a rich guy's house to a full-on protect Jesus himself kind of security.

On top of that, she would also find that her less than admirable contacts from her days as an operative would hire her out as a trouble-shooter for…well, for various sundry needs that corporations might encounter. She had never known calm and peaceful. Her life had always been a scratch fight, and that was what she really actually enjoyed. Even as a kid, she came from a rough and tumble family, but that was far in the past and the last thing she ever wanted to talk about.

She had spirit, and she meant well in all her intentions—well, almost all of them. Beneath the strong but feminine muscles, the unyielding stare, and the no-nonsense personality, she had a soft spot. Now, if you pointed that out, she would obviously kick your ass because when it came down to it, she had faced some of the scariest and most notorious killers in history and walked out alive. She wasn't about to take shit from anyone else.

When she got out of the businesses she'd been in, she virtually had a laundry list of aliases she could go by. When she started out, she had simply used her name, but that wouldn't fly, at least not for long. So when she left the operations business, she'd had the boss "kill her off" so no one would come looking for her. As could be imagined, she had been more than startled to have ONE R&D figure out who she actually was and hunt her down. The job was so interesting, though, and she found herself so intrigued with what they needed her to do, that she couldn't even start to be mad at them for it. She didn't think there were jobs left out there that could even start to catch her attention anymore. That was until Burt, the guy on the phone, had made contact with her.

A part of her hoped beyond hope that this wasn't the start of the movie-like uprising of the artificial intelligence with designs to enslave the human race. Then again, most of them probably deserved it. But so far, no one had asked her to do anything wild like keep someone in a cage in bondage, so she had decided to run with it to see where it took her.

Her mission on that particular day was actually really simple. She had to hire Stephanie. The interview, really, was like a show. The girl already had the job before she even stepped foot on the TRAM. But also, Elizabeth was responsible for testing her negotiation skills and poise because apparently, last time, she bombed that part of it hardcore.

Now, she rubbed her hands together. "So, are you enjoying your time in DC so far?"

Stephanie kept her poise and responded with a small flash of a smile. "It's very nice. I appreciate all the effort to make sure that I am comfortable here."

Elizabeth put her hands down. "Good. I'm glad. Now, we will go through a couple of tests. They won't be pod driven but will be 3D real-life thought processes."

The girl nodded and rested her hands in her lap. The older woman stood and slammed both hands on the tabletop and pulled them up slowly. The 3D imaging followed her and created a bubble that floated between them. Stephanie chuckled at how hard she had jumped.

The executive typed on the table top, and Stephanie quickly realized it had computer touch technology in the surface of it. "Okay. I put fifteen scenarios that cover morality, Meligorn tradition, and decision processing. Go through each one and select the multiple choice you think is best. If, for some reason, you think you have a better idea, you can choose the other tab and type in your answer. You have twenty-two minutes. And go."

Elizabeth stood and began to wander around, peeking over at her as she worked. Unbeknownst to her or anyone else, BURT had already set Stephanie up with additional training. Of course, she took all the courses that everyone had seen and knew about, but a few more had been added since he knew how smart she was.

In the end, it was no contest. She had passed every single one of them. He had even calculated the results himself, especially since on ten out of fifteen questions, she had chosen other and actually written a viable possibility of an alternate solution. It was brilliant and even Elizabeth could see it in her. She was no ordinary girl. There was something deeper in there, but the other woman couldn't quite put her finger on it.

"So," Elizabeth affirmed. "You obviously passed with flying

colors. Congrats. So, before I move forward, I want to ask—is this a company you would like to work for?"

Stephanie glanced around and the corner of her mouth tugged upward. "I think most definitely. It has all the qualities that are essential to research and development without all the annoyances that usually go along with that. So, yes. I would love to."

Elizabeth smiled and grabbed two rubber-tipped pens and tossed her one. She cleared the scenario on the tabletop in front of her and brightened the tone to create a writing pad. "Now, all we have to do is negotiate the salary. I will write the initial offer and we can go from there."

She held back a smirk as she wrote down the very slap-in-the-face original offer of twenty-K in credits and room and board. Without a word, she flipped the virtual paper and slid it toward Stephanie. She watched her face carefully, but the girl didn't even blink. Elizabeth was almost fearful that she would have to be the one to slap the hell out of her for accepting an offer that wasn't even appropriate for a janitor.

To her surprise and pleasure, though, Stephanie looked at her. "Okay, I see you made the first move. Now, why don't we get the laughs out of our system and start the actual negotiation?"

The woman licked her lips and managed not to grin. "Counter me."

Stephanie began writing without even a pause to think. Either she had planned it before, or she was so genius she had it on lock. She finished and flipped the paper to push it back across the table.

Elizabeth took a deep breath and voiced it out loud. "Your counter is two hundred and fifty thousand dollars, room and board, transportation, a pod in your room, retirement plan and… a three-year minimum of three hundred and fifty thousand dollars should you be let go for any reason."

That right there was her leftover trauma from what had

happened to her. And the fact that she wanted to keep herself moving forward, not be caught up in the money for the long term. Elizabeth rubbed her hand over her mouth and tried to hide the shock on her face. She had seen her one and raised by one hundred and eighty thousand dollars per year, a pod, retirement, and a clause that would make her even richer than when she was working if she were to be discharged for any reason. That was brilliant.

In all reality, as Elizabeth tapped her fingers over the paper, she wasn't nervous in the least. What she had offered was actually still a little lower than what she was worth but not as low as she'd expected. So of course, Elizabeth immediately became competitive. She was determined to win this contract war, and at the same time, do what she was there to do—train her.

They went back and forth several times, Elizabeth basically trying to take as much away from it as possible without losing it. She wanted to see how far someone could push her before she reached her breaking point. But with each negotiation, Stephanie stayed cool and composed, countered it with very little change, and in fact, at one point, started to push her price up.

Elizabeth put her hands in the air and laughed. "That's more than your original. That's two hundred and seventy-five thousand dollars, room and board, transportation, a pod in your room, retirement plan, and your three hundred and fifty thousand a year if you are fired."

Stephanie nodded. "That sounds about right. I realized when I came in here that I would let it all go and know my worth. Well, as we went along, I let go of that feeling of not wanting to talk about money out of insecurity. And when I did that, I realized that I am still discounting myself and my abilities. I would be an asset, not a depreciation."

The older woman was impressed but still reluctant to give in, so she pulled the oldest trick in the book. "I totally think you're worth it, but I'm not allowed to go that high for this position. It's really the limits that were put on us. We all have to answer to someone and basically, I am only the negotiator. How about this? How about we start you lower at say, one hundred and twenty thousand a year—"

Stephanie folded her arms. "Okay. How about I walk?"

Elizabeth tried to play it tough and threw her hands up like there was nothing she could do. The girl stared at her for a second before she slid her hand into her pocket. She put her phone on the table and spun it around a couple of times. "It's obvious that you have missed the whole point of the fact that I will not sell myself short. But hey. I have another option. It just so happens that I have Ambassador V'ritan's number memorized. I have his permission to contact him at any time. I'm sure he would like to have someone like me on his staff while he is here on Earth. I know the Meligornians are rolling in the Federation's money and because they are not a commerce kind of planet, they have more than enough to go around. He'd probably double my original proposal."

BURT watched the camera feed and listened to her use her clout and her self-confidence to push the envelope on the discussions. He could see Elizabeth grind her teeth and try to see if she was bluffing or not. The woman had no idea that BURT had made sure she would be on the TRAM with V'ritan. After a couple of minutes had passed, Elizabeth shook her head, placed her palms on the surface, and pulled the images down to the center of the tabletop.

She chuckled as she leaned back and rolled her neck. "That's really cute. Nice touch, really but...uh, we both know you don't have his number. But it was a good try, seriously."

Stephanie sat there with a small, almost condescending smile on her face. She didn't think of it that way, though. Surprisingly, she really enjoyed negotiating for her salary. She liked the small trace of irritable tension between the two of them as they basically scrutinized one another and tried to decide if the other was bullshitting them or not. In this case, Stephanie already knew she wasn't attempting something that she couldn't follow through on and in her mind, that gave her the controlling hand.

She tapped her phone to turn the screen on. "Here's a deal. I call him—the ambassador, that is. If either he or his guard Brilgus answers, I get what I want on the first bid from me. Two hundred and fifty thousand and all the rest I originally put down. Let's be honest. I know I'm worth more than that, but I like this place. I like the feel of it, the way that it's so simplistic on the outside and so technologically beyond where we are out there on the inside. It's camouflaged, basically. And there aren't a million employees coming and going and making everything a huge mess from the beginning."

"And if you don't win?"

Stephanie shrugged. "Then I have to compromise. If I don't win, we agree to your numbers for six months and I'm out of the contract if I'm not worth the money. Or, we agree to move to my numbers. It will be a back to the drawing board kind of thing. What do you think?"

Elizabeth stretched her arms over her head and leaned back as she sucked air through her teeth. "I don't know…that's not a lot of compromise. If you lose, run with my offer for six months, with a fifty percent raise thereafter. At eighteen months, if we still have you under contract, we will agree to your full requests. No questions asked. We can even draw them up now and secure them in a nice little glass case waiting for you to break the glass and get your just rewards. That is more like a compromise in my eyes."

She stared at her opponent for a minute and without saying anything, picked her phone up. Her heart thudded a little, but she closed her eyes to bring the vivid picture of the ambassador's information to the forefront of her mind. When she had it, she typed in the contact information and pressed send. Finally, she had to type in her very long ID number that he had given on the card. All the while, Elizabeth simply sat and watched and shook her head.

Stephanie set the phone on the table facing her as she waited for the system to clear her ID number. BURT found it almost comical how they both sat there and stared at each other, both with a smirk on their faces but neither with raised or heightened emotions. They were simply two high-powered women who both tried to have their way. They were so cunning that something like that could last way longer than an afternoon in the warehouse.

The phone beeped twice and began to ring. One ring... Two rings...

CHAPTER TWENTY-TWO

"Hello, this is Ambassador V'ritan's number, Brilgus speaking. Who is this?"

Elizabeth raised an eyebrow, not fully convinced yet.

Stephanie smirked and leaned forward. "Hello, Brilgus, this is Stephanie from the TRAM yesterday."

Immediately, the guard's voice went from gruff to warm and inviting. "Oh, hi, Steph! I guess you saw the news. The ambassador was sad he couldn't share who he was with you. He really was enjoying your open conversation and he knew that would change the whole thing. Of course, he also tries to keep a low profile and no matter how well we vet those trains, we are never fully sure that they aren't bugged in some way."

She grinned. "Please, no apologies are ever needed to me. I'm actually the one who should be apologizing."

"Why?" he asked. "You were on point with everything and you were able to calm your excitement down quicker than I would have if I were in your shoes."

Stephanie laughed. "I just pictured you as a giggling school girl. No, I realized, when I saw him on the news, that I didn't bow correctly to him. He's on the level of royalty and I should never have grasped his arm."

Brilgus laughed and waved her off. "He doesn't do anything he doesn't want to do, trust me. He was so impressed that you even knew what to do there, and on top of that, speaking to him in Meligornian, that was sweet. I won't lie, I was impressed."

She shared his amusement briefly before she took a deep breath. "I don't want to hold you up, but I thought I would call and offer to take you and the ambassador to dinner while we are in DC."

The guard groaned. "I wish we could. I really do apologize but he is booked solid for the next month. In fact, there are days where he is having dinner twice in one night. It's exhausting and insane. However, I do suspect he would rather cancel some of the dinners and spend more time with you discussing Meligorn theory than business contracts between worlds."

They both laughed while Elizabeth sat and listened quietly. Stephanie tapped her fingers on the glass and watched curiously as small bubbles of color appeared and disappeared with each tap. "Well, Brilgus, it was great talking to you. I'll let you get back to protecting and serving. I'm sorry you are stuck at all the boring stuff out there. Know I'll be thinking about you while I enjoy my free time."

He chuckled. "Thanks for that. You take care and don't hesitate to call if you need anything."

Stephanie put her finger on the phone. "Will do. Bye."

She pressed the off button and leaned back in her chair, a triumphant smile on her face. "There you go. I think that was more than enough information for you to be convinced it was really him."

Elizabeth clapped her hands. "I have to admit, I'm not stupidly shocked—you are a bright girl—but I am a bit surprised. I think anyone would be. But I guess you got your way."

Stephanie pumped her fist and cleared her throat as she straightened in the chair again. "I have to pass my finals, of course. But I can start after that if you wish."

The older woman took a deep breath, swiped the tabletop computer off, and chuckled to herself. "It's the first time I've been bested that badly in eighteen years. For eighteen long years, I have been on a winning streak."

"What happened eighteen years ago?"

Elizabeth stood and pushed in her chair, and her eyes glistened with the memories of eighteen years before. She shifted her gaze to meet Stephanie's. The girl's eyebrow was raised, and her arms folded. Elizabeth pointed at her and paused for a moment. "Ask me again when you're twenty-one. It's not a story meant for the faint of heart, that's for sure." She cracked up and shook her head. "Oh, man. Okay, there is one more thing to do and then you can head out and enjoy your night in DC."

Stephanie followed her, feeling a whole lot of relief that the hard and anxiety-ridden part of it was over. She hadn't known what to expect when she came out there, but it wasn't nearly as scary as she thought it would be.

Elizabeth led her down a long hall, painted completely dark-gray from floor to ceiling with a faint glow to it. She reached a large steel door and leaned forward to enter a code. A box hissed forward, and the doors slid open. The woman set her chin on the holder and stared directly ahead as the machine scanned her retina. She pulled back and blinked for a moment until it shut. A small keyboard-looking device popped out and she pressed her finger onto the circle. Stephanie heard a small burst of air and Elizabeth moved to the edge of the board and dripped a small bead of her blood on it.

She looked at Stephanie as it ran her information. "This one is kind of the crowning jewel if you can't tell."

Stephanie chuckled as the door unlocked and Elizabeth pulled it open. As they stepped out onto the white floor, the tiles lit up with each step. 3D images hovered all around the edges, some of them full bodies and others digital representations of a person's heart, lungs, and veins. In the center was a pod, painted in a bright blue, the door already open.

Elizabeth put her hands out. "These are the representations of your stats. No more tiny screens. This is your pod."

The girl pointed at it in bemusement and approached it nervously. "Wow. This is unlike anything I've seen before."

"Because it was made especially for you."

Stephanie wanted to ask how, since she'd only just gotten the job, but she was too eager to jump in and get going so she brushed it off as more of an overstatement then the actual truth. Elizabeth took her envelope and bag and set it on a clean white table. "In this one, you have to go in naked. That's part of the reason why I am the one who was chosen to be here and do this with you. That and the fact that I am supremely qualified. Sorry, boys, no need to apply."

She laughed nervously and turned away as she began to take her clothes off. While she was extremely shy, she pushed through it as fast as she could. She folded her clothes and set them on the table. As she climbed into the pod, she glanced quickly at her companion and realized that Elizabeth had actually turned away to give her privacy.

"This pod is engineered for continuous use. It can sustain you for almost a full month should something happen. If there is a power outage, we don't want you to be stuck in there without provision," the woman explained.

Stephanie was shocked. She had never heard of something like that. Sure, it was nuts that it could do that, but even more so that there was some sort of mechanism that would be deployed that would be able to keep her alive for up to a month if she was offline from everyone. *Shit, how advanced is this pod?*

Elizabeth walked over as she lay down and looked at the simple but sleek interior. "The main concern for this, and why so many precautions were taken, is because of your power. If your research breaks something, the company has time to figure out how to pull you out safely. But, it's only a safety feature. We don't actually expect that to ever happen. We merely want to be prepared."

She raised her eyebrow and glanced at Elizabeth's middle as she stood with her hands on the door. Instinctively, she looked around her for buttons, gloves, or headpieces, but there was nothing—only a small touch screen in the front with the ONE R&D logo on it and that was it. "There is no need for me to adjust anything?"

The woman chuckled as if she sensed her disbelief and didn't blame her. It was beyond wild. "Steph, relax. This is a very special pod."

Stephanie mumbled nervously to herself, "Right, right. Made especially for me, got it."

Elizabeth tapped the door. "I'm gonna send you in for only a few. We want to make sure everything is connected properly. So, go in the world, do something small and not too fancy, and then tell the AI you want to come back. It's that simple."

She gave her a thumbs-up and rested her hands on her stomach as she shut the door. A stream of sparkling lights shimmered on the ceiling which provided enough light to make it comfortable. Beneath her and within the cushioning of the bed, a small needle pricked her on the ass cheek. It wasn't enough to make her jump, but she definitely noticed. Quickly, though, the warming of the bed liner and the serum injected took her into the Virtual World.

The avatar room revealed no surprises and she took a deep breath realized that she was at least in her panties and bra now. She hastily tapped a pair of jeans, a hoodie, and some flip flops.

When she was done, she glanced upward as she usually did to look for the AI even although, in reality, they were all around her. Without a word, mostly because Stephanie had become something of a pro at it, she zoomed out and appeared in a field of tall, waving grass on Meligorn.

Her neck felt a little stiff which was strange since she was only an avatar, but everything also felt like it moved much quicker as far as processing speeds went. That, she wouldn't complain about. After a hurried look around, she grabbed a piece of tall grass and broke it off. "Something quick…something quick. Okay."

She gripped the piece of grass in her hand and closed her eyes to draw the energy up and through her. A surge struck her hard in the chest and almost knocked her off her feet. She opened her eyes and glanced around. That had been much harder than it usually was. Nonetheless, she could still feel the magic flowing through her.

Stephanie focused on the piece of grass and pushed magic through her fingertips and over the blade. Then, without a question in her mind, she tossed it into the air and watched as it burst and transformed into a hundred different butterflies that swooped and swirled around her. She laughed and found solace in her abilities. If only she could stay longer, but she had her instructions. Besides, she would be back soon.

"I'm ready to go back," Stephanie called to her AI.

The AI replied, "Close your eyes."

She obeyed instantly and waited a moment until her cool hand touched the bare skin of her belly. Just like that, she was back—no soaring scenes and no white room. Merely in and out, like walking through a door. The door hissed and opened slowly. She covered her breasts and locked her knees as she slid out. Elizabeth had her head turned away and held her clothes up.

"Thanks." Stephanie chuckled, took them, and pulled them on quickly.

She zipped her dress and tapped Elizabeth on the shoulder. The woman turned and stuck her hand out to shake Stephanie's. "Welcome to ONE R&D. As long as you can get back within a month, we are good."

While that weighed slightly on her mind, it was more of a nail-biter than a complete freak-out session. She merely needed to make sure to focus herself and get shit done. It was definitely worth it. Elizabeth looked at her watch and clapped firmly before she led her out of the room. She locked it and pressed a code to arm the security on it. "It's 2:54. Perfect timing. Do you need me to walk you out?"

Stephanie looked straight down the hall to the lobby door. "Nope. I guess I work here now so I got it."

Elizabeth snapped her fingers. "We'll see you tomorrow, kiddo. And no need to dress up. Be comfortable, girl."

She chuckled and thought about all the clothes she'd bought. When she walked outside, her limo driver was already waiting, his arms out and his eyes wide. She giggled and gave him a thumbs-up. He gave her a high-five and opened the door. She climbed in, happy to take her heels off and put her feet up. Once she'd wiggled into a comfortable position, she grabbed her phone from her bag and frowned at a missed text. It was an alert from her bank to notify her that she had to come in to sign some documents.

"Weird...maybe they are already processing me a bonus. Sweet." She tossed it back in her purse.

Back at the building, Elizabeth hurried to her office and created a report to send to the owner. She knew he'd already crept in on them anyway, but she intended to follow all the way through. Once she'd sent the report off, she grabbed her jacket and purse, flipped her light off, and locked the door. As she headed down the hall, she turned the light switches off and pulled out her keys. She locked the inside door, pulled it twice to check, and then made her way to the security board, where she punched in her key and pressed arm.

An eye-roll was not even sufficient for the lackluster security system they had on the place. "I really need to upgrade that POS," she muttered to herself as she left.

A hoverbike turned the corner and came to a stop on the other side of the street from the warehouse complex. The driver kept his helmet on, the visor down to hide his eyes. He watched as the limo pulled out and sped off with Stephanie Morgana inside. He was about to turn the bike on again but paused as another woman came out the front doors and locked them behind her.

The man drew a small tablet from his back pocket and scanned through the ambassador's schedule but there was no free time for a review. He scrolled through the contacts and hit send, then held it up to the now open visor of his helmet. "Yeah. Yeah, she was here. And another woman, but only those two. I thought that since the ambassador won't be open for review tonight, I'd get some tools and do a little recon. Find out what the hell they were doing inside an old dusty warehouse."

The control agreed. "Just go ahead and do it. No need to wait for dark."

"Roger that."

He turned the phone off, started his bike, and headed off to collect his tools.

Ambassador V'ritan walked out of the meeting holding his books to his chest and with his robe hood still up. He grumbled to himself as he approached Brilgus. "Pompous idiots. How has this species survived as long as it has?"

The guard toned his smile down and led the ambassador down the hall and into a private conference room. Once there, he smiled from ear to ear. V'ritan narrowed his eyes and threw up a spell of silence to hover like a shield around them. "Spill it. Why are you smiling so much?"

Brilgus chuckled. "Stephanie called. She saw you on the news and her biggest concern was that she didn't greet you properly. She wanted to take us to dinner, but she understood why we couldn't. Also, she wanted to thank us for being so awesome."

V'ritan couldn't help but smile too. He patted his companion on the back. "Thanks. I needed that to let me know this isn't a world completely full of stupidity. Only the asshats in that room." Then he paused, glancing up at Brilgus's face. "Look after her for me, okay? Let's keep her safe."

Although he hadn't planned on waiting that long, after seeing how many people lived near there, the hoverbike driver didn't return until dark. He drove past the guard shack, knowing full well if there were someone in there, they would be holographic. He hurried the bike down and around to the back of the building. At first, he'd considered the front but decided to not be so bold.

He found the electrical box and opened it to locate the wires connected to the system. With practiced ease, he plugged his small converter box into it and then to the laptop, opened it, and entered the information. Within seconds, he cracked the code and managed to turn the system off from right there. "What did they use to arm this thing? 1993 Brinks alarm? What a joke."

Still chuckling, he went to the back door, picked the lock, and strolled inside. His control watched him walk through via the camera on his helmet. He ran his finger over a shelf and sneered. "This place is clean. Too clean."

He wandered through the halls and found nothing but half-empty rooms and old offices. Finally, he ended up in front of the large steel doors. He grinned. "One of these things is not like the other."

His tools would no doubt prove their mastery once again, he thought smugly as he went to work. And tried like hell to get the door open.

CHAPTER TWENTY-THREE

The loud blare of the alarm on her tablet woke Elizabeth suddenly from her sleep. She gasped and raised her head, her hair in her eyes. For a moment, she listened into the darkness and finally realized what the sound was. She rolled over and tried to pull her leg from the covers. It got caught as she stood and threw her off balance, and she hopped and flailed across the floor. She gritted her teeth and growled loudly as she finally managed to find her feet.

Thoroughly irritated by now, she snatched the tablet off the table, swiped right, and peered at the alarm warning. "What the—"

Someone thought they were smart enough to break into the office by simply disarming the outer security system. "Little did you know, dumbass, that in itself triggers the alarm."

She was rightfully pissed, she decided as she fumbled for her clothes and pulled them on. Not only because someone actually had the nerve to try to break in, but also because the building sucked ass so badly when it came to security.

"AI, wake up," Elizabeth said and hopped around as she

attempted to pull her boot on. "Call the cops and send them to the warehouse. I'm headed over there now."

"Of course. Be safe," the AI responded.

Elizabeth laughed. "Yes, Mom, of course."

BURT worked through gathering several of the programs he had spread out during the hacking attempt back into a more secure location. He didn't want them all together but definitely couldn't leave them dangling out in other countries. That could be catastrophic. He lost focus when a notification buzzed through his system. Someone tried to force their way into his special lab.

Immediately, he was pissed beyond belief and turned his load and attention to the building. He scanned through the security camera and found the culprit right away. The man stood in front of the steel door and tried to figure out how to circumvent the single piece of security equipment. The intruder selected a different tool and resumed his attempt, whispering to himself as he worked.

He glanced at the camera but at that point, didn't seem to care. Of course, perhaps he thought he had shut them off. "There must be something inside here. The outside security was too damned easy."

BURT immediately made notes that he would need to pay a hell of a lot more attention to the shit in the real world if intended to dabble with real-world things. That included having the appropriate security for any building that he owned or rented.

Elizabeth groaned and held her hand on the horn. She looked out and down from her sky-vehicle and knew she had to shift down lanes to make sure she could take the right exit. "Hey, asshole! Try to pick up the pace instead of picking your ass!"

He flipped her off and sped away. As she made her way down the lanes of traffic, the AI in the car had a field day with all the tickets she had accrued. "We have received a ticket for excessive speeding, four hundred dollars in Federation credits or coins. Another ticket for endangering birds by leaving designated lanes, six hundred dollars in Federation credits or coins. We have received a ticket for flying on a no-fly zone and endangering the buildings and architecture through the city, two hundred dollars in Federation coins or credits."

She jerked the wheel to swerve around a car and back again. The AI spoke immediately. "A ticket for changing lanes without using a signal, two hundred dollars in Federation coins or credits. Passing on a one-way fly-way, six hundred dollars in Federation coins or credits."

Elizabeth yanked the steering wheel to circumvent the other vehicles while she screamed and went wild at the people who wouldn't let her over. The AI paused but didn't stop. "Exposing a Federation ruled breast and nipple to the public, three hundred and fifty dollars. Un-ladylike behavior regulated by the Federation: grabbing crotch and screaming out, 'Screw this little gremlin,' thirty-six dollars in Federation coins or credits."

"For God's sake! Shove the tickets up your ass and shit confetti," she yelled irritably.

The AI responded with silence. "Oh, shit!" she yelled as she yanked the wheel to the side, slammed on the brakes, and immediately pressed the accelerator again.

The intruder jimmied the security code box on the door with three new tools but still had little success. He growled in frustration and threw them in the box. "Goddamned door."

His finger was bleeding, so he sucked on the blood and stared belligerently at the door. His gaze shifted through his tools and finally slowed on the dynamite patch that protruded from his bag. A new speculative light glistened in his eyes and he packed his stuff before he removed the patch and smirked.

"For those times when a knock isn't sufficient." He chuckled.

He stared at the patch and grimaced when he remembered the last time he'd used one. It was not a pleasant memory. He had picked concrete out of his back for weeks because he hadn't run fast enough. That wouldn't happen now, though. He simply wanted to get in and out as fast as possible. He peeled the back off the patch and attached the cables to the bottom. His first instinct was to apply it to the door, but he shook his head and shifted his focus to the wall. He felt he had a better chance to get through that way than if he tried to bust through steel doors.

BURT watched what he did and began a calculation of the different odds for the likely outcome. He ran them one last time, scanned them into his system, and created the reaction that would correlate with the answers. Suddenly, he startled and turned his attention back to the camera.

>>Oh shit...

The spy hurried down the hall and around the corner, unwinding the wires as he went. He connected them to the detonation box very carefully. While he had already tucked himself safely around the corner, he really didn't want to be surprised by a loud-ass explosion. He figured he would be safe there and the rest of the debris would damage the walls or whatever. It was merely a small dynamite patch, after all.

Once everything was hooked up, he snickered to himself and flattened his back against the wall. "Fire in the hole—"

A homeless man wandered down the block, smacked his lips, and spilled the one and only bottle of whiskey he'd managed to pick up that day. As he approached the front of the warehouse area, he hiccupped and fumbled inside his jacket to pull a white cat out. It mewed and rubbed its whiskers on his face. "We're gonna get real warm tonight, Mr. Fluffy."

Suddenly, there was a huge explosion and the first building inside the warehouse area erupted in a truly magnificent blast. The homeless man fell back, landed hard, and coughed as smoke and debris filled his lungs. The blast had blown his eyebrows and Mr. Fluffy's ass hair off.

CHAPTER TWENTY-FOUR

Elizabeth gripped the steering wheel tightly and tried to fight the turbulence that threatened to jerk it from her grasp. "Come on, baby, get ahold of yourself."

The car shuddered and swerved, slewed slightly, and finally straightened. Her shoulders relaxed and she exhaled a deep breath as she regained her control again. She leaned her head down and glared out the window. A brilliant flash of light was immediately followed by a rolling cloud of smoke and fire that swelled into the night sky.

The AI came back over the speaker. "Loss of building, $1.2 million Federation credits or coins."

She rolled her eyes and hit the gas, shaking her head and mumbling, "That's what insurance is for."

Angrily, she blinked at the billowing smoke in the distance, as pissed as hell that this was how her night had ended up. After everything she had accomplished that day, this was the universe's way of saying thank you. "I'll find these asswipes and make sure to get my money back."

Her phone rang loudly in the car and she jumped and swerved to the right. She swished her hand through the air to activate the onboard phone connection. The screen read, **The Boss.**

Her nostrils flared. "Well, *shit.*"

The cheerful chirping of birds and light strumming of a harp pumped quietly through Stephanie's hotel apartment. Very slowly, the light brightened the room, and a scene of shimmering wheat fields covered all the walls. She rolled over in bed and stretched her arms overhead. A tremor of anticipation pushed through her and she smiled for a moment before she groaned and snuggled in for another minute.

"Good morning, Stephanie. How did you sleep?" the AI asked.

She grinned. "Like a baby with a brand-new lucrative career and a bed made from the clouds of heaven. So, pretty good."

The AI paused. "You have a new message on your tablet. Sender is ONE R&D."

Stephanie opened her eyes and snatched her tablet from the side table. She swiped left and opened the message screen, still astounded at how fast the Net was in the hotel. The message was from Elizabeth and she clicked on it immediately.

Stephanie, your day at ONE R&D has been canceled due to lack of access to the building. Any and all training will be made up on your first day reporting for the job. As you are already in Washington and don't leave on the TRAM until tomorrow, we have deposited funds into your account so that you are able to do anything you would like to in the city today. Have fun and stay safe. We will be in contact soon. -Elizabeth.

She pursed her lips and put the tablet down. On one hand, she had never seen DC before, but on the other, she really wanted to spend some time in the Virtual World. A little disappointed now, she pulled the covers back and hopped out of bed to wander into the dining area.

"I took the liberty of ordering you your favorite breakfast and the coffee is steaming hot," the AI informed her.

Stephanie smiled and sat on one foot in the chair. She took a bite of bacon. "Thanks, Sarah. Will you alert the limo driver that I will be ready to go in an hour?"

"Sure. Where is your destination? The remnants of the monument? The foundation of the White House? The shrine to the Third World War?"

She shook her head. "No, only to the local pod rental place. At least to start with."

Her mind made up, she hurried through breakfast and stood for a moment as she considered her clothes. She didn't want to wear anything special as she'd prefer to keep a low profile so simply threw on a pair of jeans, a hoodie, and a new pair of running shoes she had asked Sarah to have sent up. It took barely a moment to pull her hair into a ponytail and put a baseball cap on.

The limo driver was more than happy to take her to a pod place, but instead of the closest, he took her to the nicest one. That way, she could also see the new reflecting pool they had built. It was the fifth one and included holographic images of DC historical features that traced peacefully over the water. It was nice enough, but Stephanie's mind was on the pod.

He dropped her there and circled the block to find parking. She didn't have any issues, and no one seemed to pay any attention to who she was. Better yet, she definitely wasn't recognized by anyone. The guy at the front was surprised that she wanted the best pod in the private room, but money talked, and she had more than enough. He took her back and reprogrammed the palm security for the door so that she would be the only one to be able to access it when she was in there.

Once inside the rig, she put the gloves on and the sensors on her head and recalled how amazing it had been in the other pod. While she wasn't sure how this one worked, it was still awesome.

She stood in the avatar closet room and scrolled through the bank robber game weapons. The batteries were not in stock and the note in their place claimed some sort of system malfunction. Instead, she chose a laser gun and two electric daggers and suited up. When she pressed the button, she was transported instantly to the non-magical side. She immediately began to run through and fired an ongoing barrage at the enemies.

Three men waited directly ahead of her, ready to fire as soon as she came within range. She threw herself aside and flipped onto a two-foot-wide ledge. As she began to slide along on her back, she aimed her weapon out between her legs. She pulled the trigger and struck the first attacker squarely in the chest to catapult him back over the railing to the level below. Shifting her aim, she fired at the second and grimaced as his head erupted a split second before his body folded in almost slow motion. She turned her sights on the third but had reached the end of the ledge and fell to land hard and roll awkwardly. Her head bounced off one of the chairs in the terminal waiting area and she groaned as she rubbed the back of it.

The sound of a cocking gun made her open her eyes and she sighed as she stared down the barrel of the third man's gun. "Seriously?

Pain seared through her as the bullet pierced her chest and the room hurtled out of sight. When the sense of motion ceased, she opened her eyes, snarled her annoyance, and stared at the closet ceiling. She patted her chest but there was no wound. Grimly determined, she pushed to her feet, snatched up a new gun, and pressed the button again. She landed in the same spot as before and immediately readied her weapon. A monstrous roar from her right sent a shaft of trepidation through her. A massive creature she had never seen before swiped its huge tentacle down and dashed the gun from her hands.

With a muttered curse, she made a run for it. Her legs pedaled furiously but she had barely taken a few steps when the tentacle wrapped around her ankles. Her eyes widened and her arms flailed as she fell forward, and her face smacked painfully into the floor. She groaned as blood trickled out of her mouth and into a puddle under her chin. The tentacles yanked to haul her back toward the creature. Stephanie managed to flip onto her back and scrabbled frantically to draw her two electrical knives. She grunted and forced herself to sit up as she slid toward the beast.

With both hands, she stabbed the blades into the tentacles and whipped her arms outward to cut through the flesh until the appendage was completely severed. Quickly, she yanked the dead part off her legs and bolted to her feet to make a run for the other side in search of the stairwell down to the magical area. As she sprinted over bodies on her approach to the stairs to the right, her foot landed in a pool of blood and the other one never hit the ground. She skated across the floor on a direct trajectory with the huge plate glass window up ahead. Unable to stop her momentum, she raised her hands and turned her shoulder into the impact. The motion protected her face but did nothing to slow her headlong launch through the window that overlooked the landing area below.

The outer windows might be reinforced, but interior ones definitely were not, she thought stupidly as glass shards fell alongside her. She scowled as she registered the sting of innumerable abrasions, then stiffened as she realized her predicament. Her mind whirled as she tried to calculate the odds of surviving the fall, which didn't seem particularly good. She sniffed and grumbled her frustration and wondered how badly the impact would hurt. The mental calculation was wasted effort as she never did find out. She looked up and gasped as a ship slammed into her.

Stephanie sat straight on the floor, her breath rasping, and clutched her chest. She was in the avatar closet once more, mended and ready to go again. She struggled to her feet, placed her hands on her back, and cracked it. "Ughhh."

Absolutely enraged now, she stumbled over to the wall and grabbed two pistols, a dagger, and a laser gun this time. She would go full Rambo and didn't give a rat's ass. Her fist pounded the go button and she appeared in the back corner of the sixth-floor non-magic side. That meant she had to make it down three floors simply to find the robbers in the first place. With a sigh that she hoped would calm her a little, she drew her pistol and immediately whipped it up to shoot a man in the face. She stepped over his body, stopped, and waited for two people with chainsaws—she had no idea where they found those—to run past, screaming at one another. A part of her wondered if this game was more of an excuse to run around in crazy avatars with stupid weapons than to actually stop bank robbers.

Nonetheless, she continued and eliminated four people and a huge owl before she reached the stairwell. She hurried down, skipped floors five and four, and took two steps at a time until she landed at floor three. She had no desire to go in and simply wanted to make it to the magical side, but as she passed the door, she heard men yelling to get down on the ground.

As she paused there, she heard another one. "Put the money in the bag!"

"The robbers," she whispered quietly.

She checked the mags in her pistols to confirm she had one bullet left in one and nine in the other. Her daggers were still strapped to her sides and the laser gun lay comfortably on her back. She crept up to the stairwell door and peeked out through the crack. Across the hall was the First Federation Bank and sure enough, the simulated bank robbery was in progress. The whole point of the game was to get the bank robbers to the magical prison before getting killed by someone or something.

Stephanie crouched and crept through the door to take cover behind a half wall. Slowly, she peeked over the top and watched as the robbers hustled out. There were only two. Both wore clown masks and carried the money stuffed in duffel bags. She moved her fully loaded pistol to her left hand and held the laser gun in the right. She took a deep breath, stood, and aimed at the men.

"Freeze. Don't move!" One of the two tried to escape but she shot him in the leg, and he tumbled amidst vociferous curses.

She stepped out from behind the wall and kicked the downed man's gun out of reach. Surprisingly, when she aimed her pistol in the other one's face, he simply assumed a slightly dazed look and began to laugh loudly. Spit dribbled out the bottom of his mask. She ripped it off, threw it to the ground, and raised her pistol to press it against his head. "It said I can win the game whether you're alive or dead."

"What did it say about you being alive or dead?" a voice said from behind her.

She put her hands up when she felt the barrel of a gun press against the back of her head. "Damnit!"

The blast of the gun echoed through her head and so did the wave of pain. When she opened her eyes in the avatar closet this time, though, she had a plan. The robbers were avatars, merely simulations, and the robbery took place at the same time and the same spot every round of the game. It was how the simulation worked. All the live players were what really made it challenging.

Stephanie selected the pistols again, some extra ammo, and a set of throwing stars. She hit the button and found herself on level four, only one up from the robbery. More carefully this time, she crept through the level and eliminated three people before she reached the stairwell. The stairs were empty so she snuck down and stopped outside the level-three door, pulled back, and aimed her gun at the place they would walk into. Sure enough, two minutes later, they came through.

Without warning, she shot the smaller one in the head and kicked his body down the steps. She looked at the other and nodded. "Throw your gun down."

He sighed and obeyed. She grabbed him hard by the neck and

stuck the gun into his back. "Don't stop until we reach the magic level."

At level zero, they stopped when they were suddenly surrounded by four guys. Stephanie shifted her gaze back and forth as they closed in on her. As soon as the first one lurched forward, she launched herself up and onto the robber's shoulders. She swung her foot into the first man's face, using his speed against him. Bones cracked and he shrieked and clutched his nose and cheeks.

Stephanie threw herself back and landed hard but immediately raced at the second of the four men. He tried to punch her, but she ducked and came up under his chin with her fist driving the thrust. Teeth flew from his mouth and his eyes rolled back as he went down. Without looking, she could feel another hurtle in from behind. She waited until he put his arms around her before she drove her elbow hard into his stomach. He gasped, winded, and she grabbed him by the head and flipped him onto his back. She shot him in the chest before he could recover and wiped her face on the back of her arm.

The fourth man had taken hold of the robber and the two raced away. She flung herself in pursuit, fired her pistols at them, and missed as they zigzagged through the station. They disappeared and reappeared in her line of sight as she took the turn wide and barreled down the steps after them. She slowed at one point and looked over the edge to estimate the jump—the height was better than her previous fall, but she might break her leg. Still, at that point, she wouldn't catch him anyway. She backed up and ran forward, grabbed the railing, and launched herself over.

She fell hard and fast but kept her arms tucked and her body ready as the ground hurtled toward her. The men looked at her and stopped to watch with wide eyes as she rocketed downward. "This was a bad idea."

Her shoulder clipped the stairwell and she flipped a mere few feet away from impact. She closed her eyes tightly and put her arms out, ready to accept the inevitable pancake. A surge of energy bolted through her chest and stomach, and she dragged in a big, gasping breath. When she didn't feel the pain of impact, she opened her eyes cautiously. It took a moment to realize that she now hovered three feet from the platform and directly opposite the two men.

Stephanie narrowed her eyes and slapped her hand out, grasped the railing, and spun her body in a wicked arc. She kicked both targets in the back of their heads and shoved them down the rest of the steps. As she flipped her body forward, she released the magic that kept her afloat and landed between them. She holstered her pistol and looked down at the one who was not the robber. "Don't take my shit."

She thrust her arm forward, the palm outward, and sent a spear of energy toward him. It pierced his body and impaled him to the ground.

"Come here," she growled as she took the robber by the neck and dragged him onto the magic deck.

After a moment or two of searching, she finally found the Federation Police building. To get there, she had to get through a mob of gang boys who obviously waited to steal him out of her custody. With a resigned sigh, she turned to the robber and smacked her hand against his forehead to deliver enough of a jolt of energy to knock him out. The gang members began to walk toward her. She closed her eyes and drew the energy into her chest before she allowed it to seep into her whole body and radiate through every part of her.

She opened her eyes and thrust her hands out. A tidal wave of purple magic streamed from her palms. It spread out like a shock wave to sweep every one of her attackers and turn them instantly to dust. She forced her arms down and as the energy drained from her palms, she looked at the empty arena in front of her.

Smugly, she turned and took hold of the unconscious robber's shirt. "Come on, asshole. Time to go to jail."

CHAPTER TWENTY-FIVE

Stephanie smiled and tilted her head back as she climbed down off the steps of the train and out onto the platform. She was heading home, happy to see her parents and excited to tell them about everything that happened. They wouldn't believe the sum of money that she'd signed on for or the fact that she'd actually gotten her dream job. She still couldn't wrap her head around it.

As she walked toward the cars, she remembered that she first needed to go to the bank. She had a note from them to stop by as soon as possible. It was only a few blocks from the TRAM, and it wasn't even dark outside yet, so she decided it would be a nice night to go for a walk and let her mind chill out and relax. If she could even find her inward place to relax. It might simply be too much to ask. Still, it was a good anxious—an excited one.

She wandered down the street and tried to keep her bag close to her, not wanting to knock into the tons of people out and about. Her bank was on the edge of the new Chicago so there weren't many problems in the area with robbery or anything like that. On that day, she was reasonably certain that if someone tried to rob her, she would definitely use the battery her father had given her. If anyone tried anything, she'd simply blow them right on their asses. Even thinking about it made her giggle.

About a block behind and completely unnoticed by her, a man leaned against the brick wall of the building and held a paper. He glanced up inconspicuously and watched as she stopped, hesitated, and finally walked across the street and skipped into the ice cream shop.

Four men stood in the alley immediately beyond the ice cream shop, huddled together in the shadows. The tallest of them stood about six-two with dark scrappy hair and a rough, grizzled beard. He leaned closer to the other three and glanced nervously toward the street. "I'll go out and you follow me in five-second intervals and catch up."

His cohorts nodded before one raised his hand. "Any particular order?"

The first man stared at him for a moment before he slapped him on the top of the head. "I don't care what order you come in. We don't want to roll out of here in a huge group, that's all. Anyway, when it's the right time—which I will decide on my own —I'll grab her and move her. If she tries any witchy stuff, you dogpile. She can't do too much—she's too young. Plus, I don't see enough batteries on her for her to produce anything wildly huge."

The group shuffled closer to the entrance to the alley and put their backs to the wall. Their leader stood at the entrance and his gaze focused each time someone walked past. He was ready to go but didn't want to move too soon and be found out. After a few more minutes, she walked past, whistling to herself. The first man nodded to the others and stepped out, shoving his hands in the pockets of his old coat.

The other men stood there, and one counted quietly to himself. The third guy elbowed him in the chest. "Why you gotta count out loud? Now I gotta start over because I can't concentrate, you moron."

He sneered. "Sorry, he said five seconds and so I wanted to make sure it was five seconds."

The other man waved his hand and looked up at the building above them. "Hey, guys…"

The first groaned. "We've been back here for like fifteen seconds. Now what do we do?"

The third man slapped them both in the chest and pointed upward. "I don't think it's really gonna matter what you do at this point."

They looked up slowly as a stranger leapt from the balcony above and landed directly on top of them. The group tumbled like skittles. The attacker turned on the man in the middle and shoved his knee into the criminal's stomach. A full fight broke out in the alley, far enough away from the main street that no one had any idea what was going on. The unknown man swung a punch and caught another thug hard in the face. As the fist connected with his skull, a wave of purple energy shivered over his skin. His eyes rolled back, and he passed out.

"Harold—shit," the first guy growled.

He lunged at the stranger, who stepped aside, swung his arm out, and latched his hand around his throat. With superhuman strength, he lifted him high and held him there, staring at him as he flailed. The man whimpered and clawed at the restraining hand. "What do you want? We don't know you. Are you one of Butcher's guys? If so, we never meant to take that money. We'll pay it back."

The unknown man's lip twitched, and he threw the thug on the ground, pulled back slightly, and hit him with enough magic to knock him out. The third man had his hands up and backed slowly down the alley. "I don't want no trouble. Please. Those guys—they ain't even my friends. We was doing what Frank wanted us to. We were supposed to be out there with him, but we got mixed up on the counting."

Suddenly, he turned and tried to make a run for it. The stranger snapped his hand and a magical whip unfurled. The end trailed at his feet. He walked forward quickly and swung the whip back before he lashed it forward with tremendous force. It wound around the thug's neck and the stranger yanked to haul him to the ground. His head struck the dirty asphalt and he passed out with both arms sprawled on either side of his inert body.

The stranger spun in search of the last man. He was concerned so he spun a magical fireball and tossed it up and out of the alley.

Stephanie smacked her lips with real relish. She could still taste the mint chocolate chip ice cream. It had been forever since she'd had one of those, and she had felt in the mood. Suddenly, a loud crack echoed, and a ball of purple energy erupted from the alley behind her and exploded into a huge firework that sizzled earthward.

With her shoulders stiff, she whirled instinctively, and her eyes shifted from the obviously magical display to the man who stood a few feet away from her. He stared at her, his arms out and hands open. He turned and looked behind him and winced as the magic sizzled on his jacket and the back of his neck. When he realized that it had come from the alley and none of his team had followed him, he narrowed his eyes.

His lip twitched and his fists clenched. "Those Goddamned idiots. They can't even count to five and now, they're playing with some sort of magic. I'll beat every single one of them."

But first, he knew he had to get the girl. Quickly, he turned back to her and his gaze darted frantically in an effort to locate her. He smacked his fist into his palm and snarled belligerently. "Goddamnit!"

She was gone, nowhere in sight, and he had been so very close to finishing the job. He turned to look right and left one last time before he cursed and hurried toward the alley. His fury mounting, he pounded his hand against the brick wall as he turned the corner and yelled to the men. "Where the—"

A bright flash of light radiated from the alley, but no one seemed to notice. The place fell silent and people continued doing what they were in town to do. Stephanie hadn't even thought for two seconds that she would be in danger, but she was the biggest target. Whoever the guys were, though, some vigilante had intervened and eliminated them before they could touch a hair on her head. Who it was remained a serious mystery.

Stephanie was tucked in the front corner of a small boutique and used the large decorative curtains on each side of the picture storefront window to hide as she looked up and down the street. Someone had been after her, but it seemed that there also happened to be someone magical there to help as well. She had no idea what to even think at that moment. On instinct, she'd simply ducked into the first place she could find and hid. She didn't want to end up in another incident like the last one where she brought even more attention to herself. On the contrary, she tried desperately to get away from all that. That was one of the points of moving forward.

As she looked out the window, a woman's voice spoke behind her. "Excuse me, can I help you? Are you all right?"

Stephanie straightened instantly, glanced around, and realized that the boutique was actually very high-end and most of the pieces in there were things she wouldn't have ever bought before because of their price tag. She licked her lips and turned with an apology on her lips, but a familiar face cut it short before it had even begun. It was the mom of the little boy at TimeWarp that day.

The woman clamped her hand over her mouth and giggled. "Oh, my goodness, you're her!"

Stephanie grinned and glanced over her shoulder to confirm that the man had gone. "I wanted to pick out a new outfit. How is my magic friend?"

The woman chuckled. "My name is Anne and his name is Brandon. He's doing really well. He tries to think of things as beautiful and he has felt the energy whenever we go to Meligorn through the pods. He still talks about that flame, though—all the time."

As they talked, Stephanie selected a long-sleeve Henley and a fleece vest that could be worn over it for a little more warmth on the cool days. She went in the back and tried them on, then, on impulse, walked out and showed Anne. "Does it look good?"

Anne smiled sweetly and nodded. "Oh, that's on the house. You look fantastic and I can't express how much you changed my son's life. Just those kind words and him being able to see and feel the energy up close. I have to keep an eye open that he isn't trying to do it, though. Burning the house down would not be the first act of magic that would make me happy."

They both laughed and Stephanie walked with her to the accessories. She picked out a hat and a pair of glasses and looked at herself in the mirror. Once she'd checked the tags, she scrabbled in her bag and handed Anne a debit card. "These are great. I can wear this right out of here."

The woman smiled with genuine care as she ran the card and handed it back to her. Stephanie couldn't help but look at her fantastic, wide-brimmed hat and giant movie-star sunglasses. This would later be the moment that could be pinpointed as marking the beginning of her love for the fashion industry.

After several hugs and a written note for Annie's son, Stephanie left the store. She looked around to make sure no one was waiting for her. The breeze blew and she held her hand on top of her hat, glanced over, and caught her reflection in the window. She looked like she belonged in an old movie, not at all the normally normal Stephanie she had always been. In fact, she looked older, and actually very nice.

She smiled and put her hand out to call a cab.

***

"Yes," the voice said, "she is home safe. But I eliminated those who looked like they wanted to grab her. I tried to question them but none of them would offer anything—most likely because I used magic to knock them out. I'll keep her under surveillance, but it will be expensive."

"Do it," a woman's voice said. "The boss wants to make sure our most important researcher makes it to work on time."

The guy chuckled. "As always, it's good doing business with you, E."

He hung up and walked into the shadows.

On the other end, Elizabeth held the phone close to her for a moment before she turned once more and covered her nose with her black-leather-gloved hand. The insurance agents were at the warehouse, walking the burned, blackened concrete where the building had been. There was barely anything left of the special research room, which completely broke her heart. That pod had been perfect, and while she knew another would be made, it still made her sad.

Her phone rang in her pocket and she pulled it out with a

sigh. She clicked the on button and put it to her ear. "Hi, boss. It's a total loss… Yes, I can find something a lot better… No, there is no security in hiding in plain sight. We were discovered much faster than we expected."

Her head shook and she paused to look over at the rubble. "Next time, they better bring a small army."